SO-CFY-253

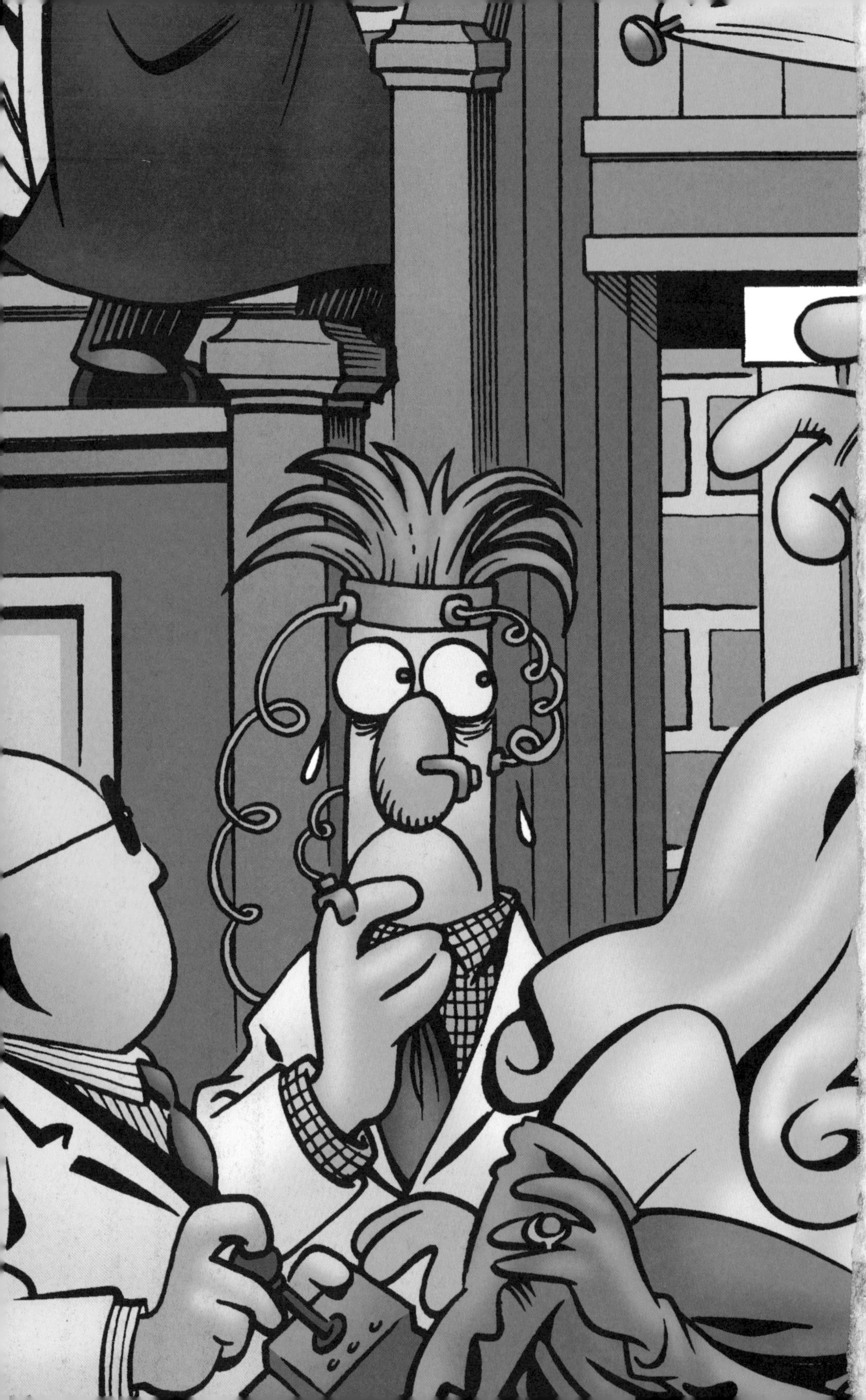

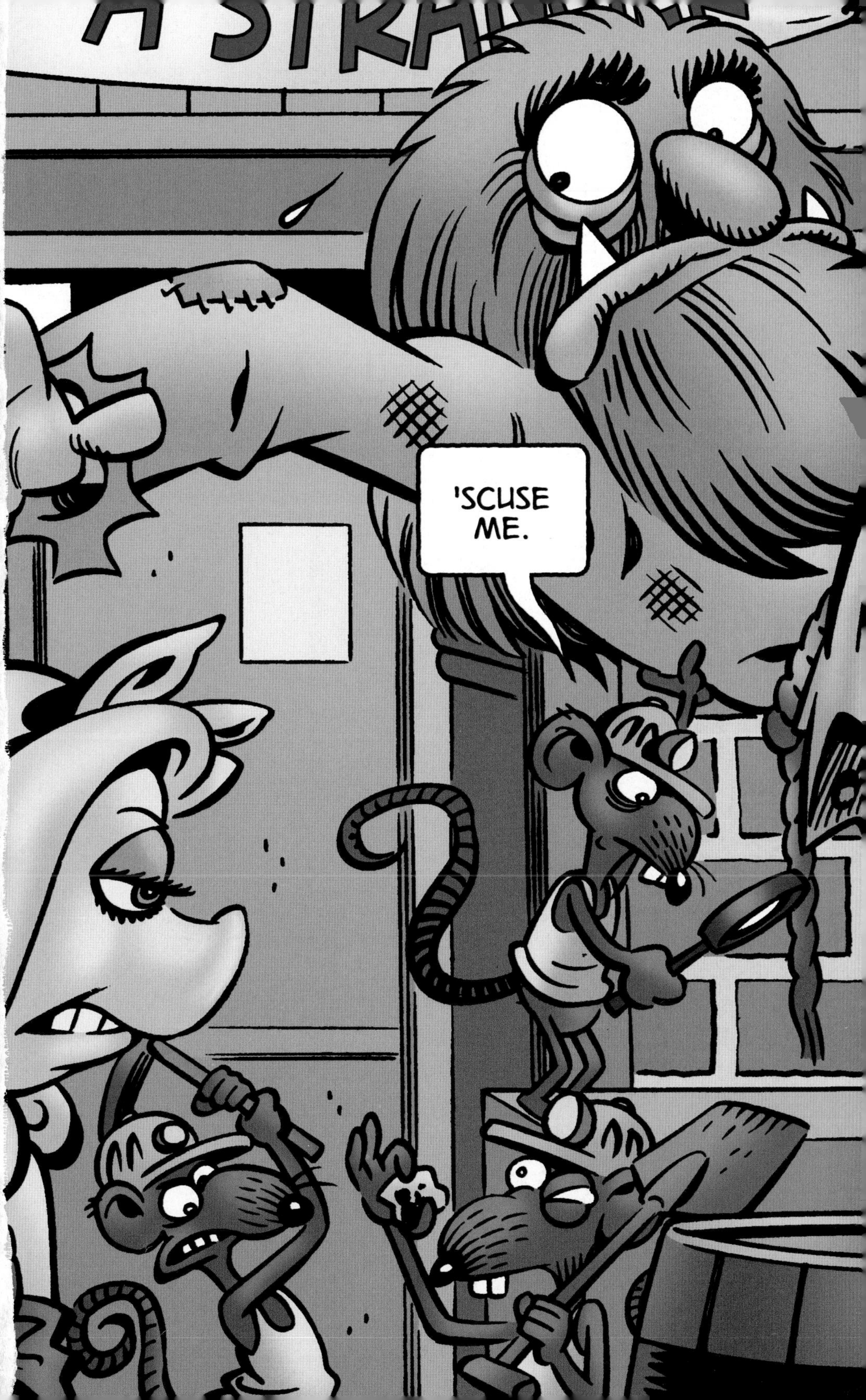
'SCUSE ME.

The MUPPET SHOW

Comic Book

BOOM Kids!

MAR 17 2010

ROSS RICHIE
chief executive officer

MARK WAID
editor-in-chief

ADAM FORTIER
vice president,
publishing

CHIP MOSHER
marketing director

MATT GAGNON
managing editor

JENNY CHRISTOPHER
sales director

FIRST EDITION: NOVEMBER 2009

10 9 8 7 6 5 4 3 2 1

PRINTED BY WORLD COLOR PRESS, INC.,
ST-ROMUALD, QC, CANADA. 12/09/09

THE MUPPET SHOW COMIC BOOK: THE TREASURE OF PEG-LEG WILSON – published by BOOM Kids!, a division of Boom Entertainment, Inc. All contents © 2009 The Muppets Studio, LLC. BOOM Kids! and the BOOM Kids! logo are trademarks of Boom Entertainment, Inc., registered in various countries and categories. All rights reserved.

Office of publication: 6310 San Vicente Blvd Ste 404, Los Angeles, CA 90048-5457.

A catalog record for this book is available from the Library of Congress and on our website at www.boom-studios.com on the Librarian Resource Page.

The Treasure
of Peg Leg Wilson

WRITTEN AND DRAWN BY **Roger Langridge**

COLORS **Digikore Studios**

LETTERS **Deron Bennett**

EDITOR **Aaron Sparrow**

COVERS **Roger Langridge**

SPECIAL THANKS: TISHANA WILLIAMS, IVONNE FELICIANO, JESSE POST, LAUREN KRESSEL, SUSAN BUTTERWORTH, JESSICA BARDWIL, JIM LEWIS AND THE MUPPETS STUDIO

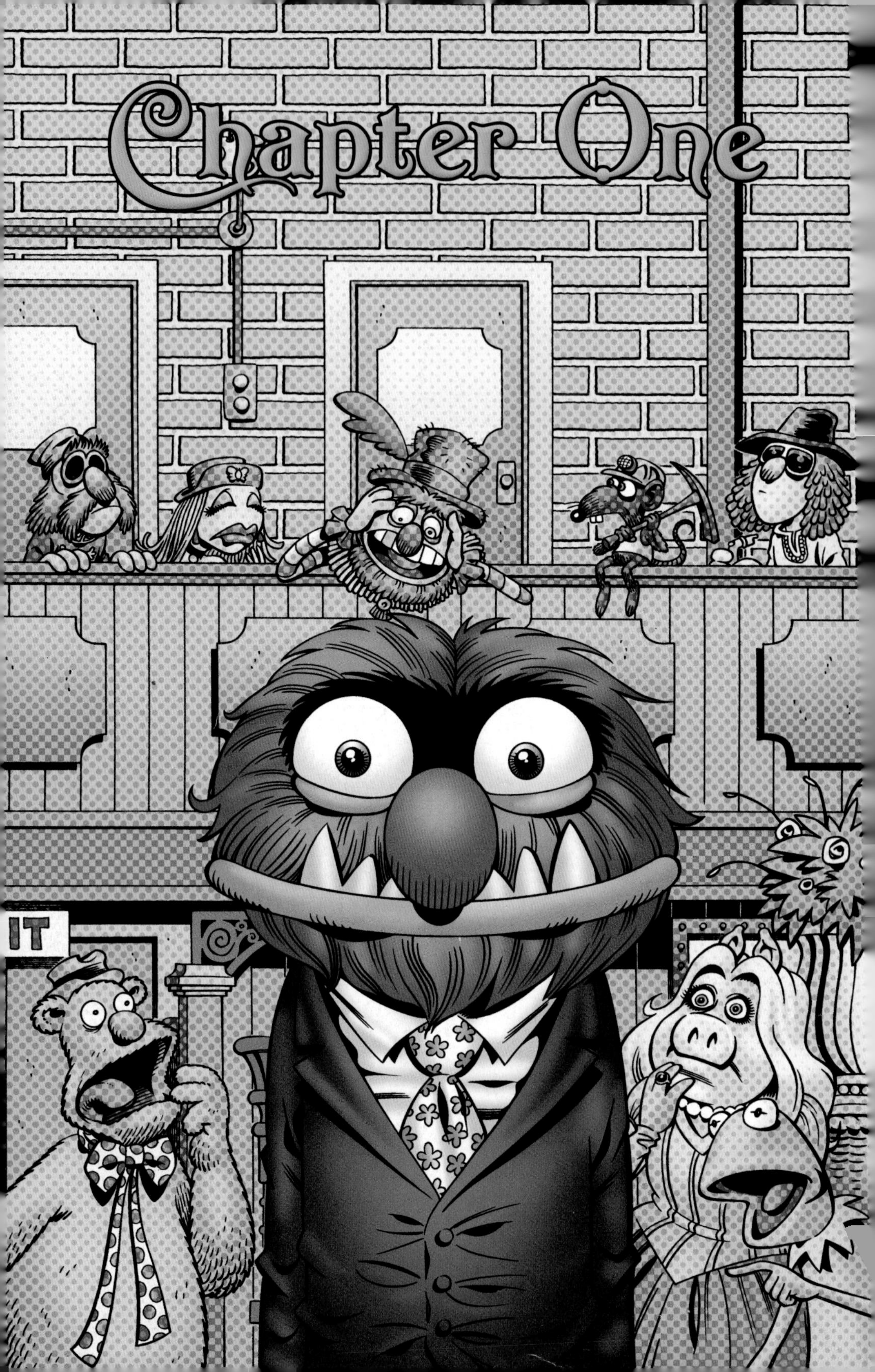
Chapter One
IT

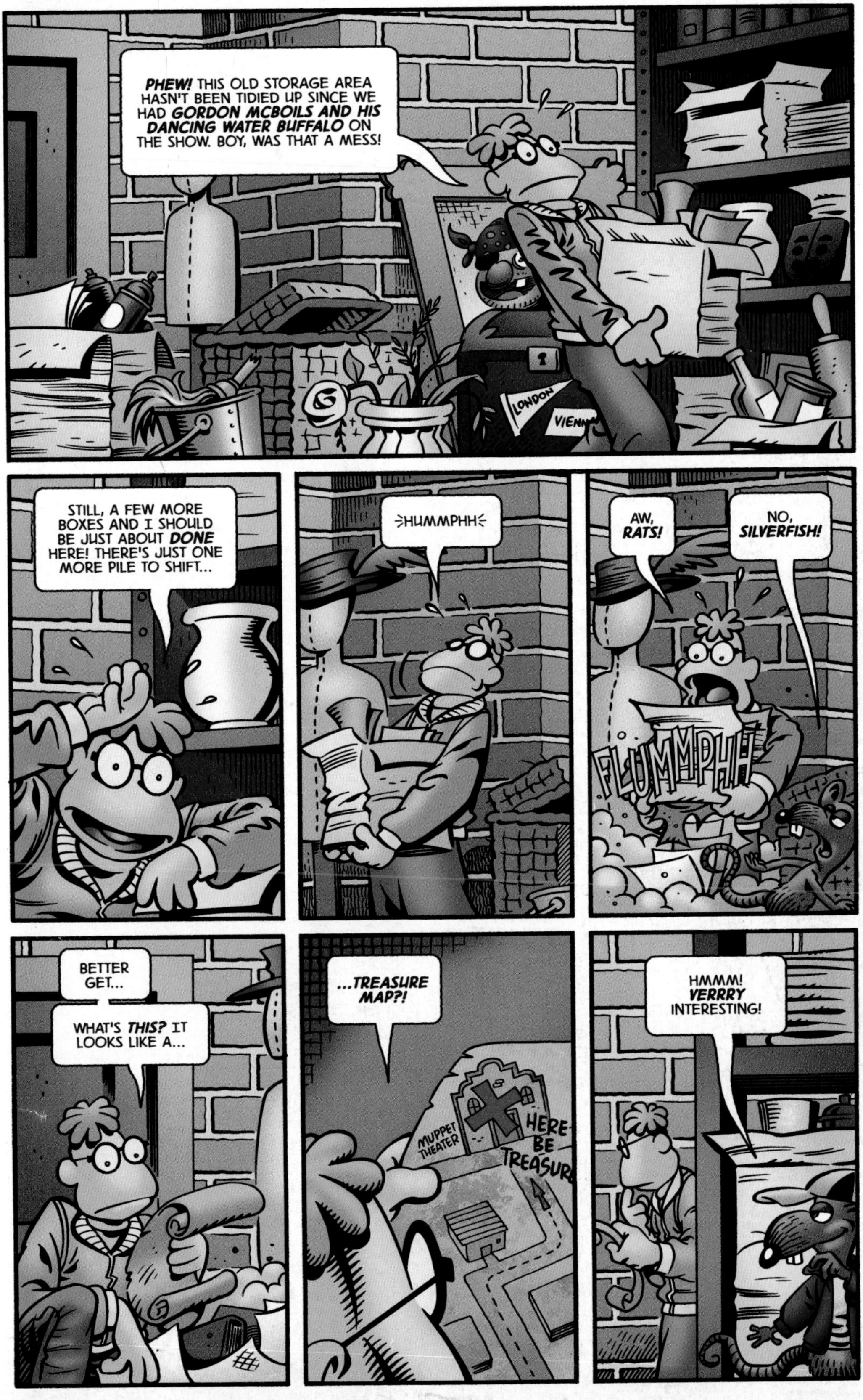
PHEW! THIS OLD STORAGE AREA HASN'T BEEN TIDIED UP SINCE WE HAD GORDON McBOILS AND HIS DANCING WATER BUFFALO ON THE SHOW. BOY, WAS THAT A MESS!
LONDON
VIENN
STILL, A FEW MORE BOXES AND I SHOULD BE JUST ABOUT DONE HERE! THERE'S JUST ONE MORE PILE TO SHIFT...
HUMMPHH
AW, RATS!
NO, SILVERFISH!
FLUMMPHH
BETTER GET...
WHAT'S THIS? IT LOOKS LIKE A...
...TREASURE MAP?!
MUPPET THEATER
HERE BE TREASURE
HMMM! VERRRY INTERESTING!

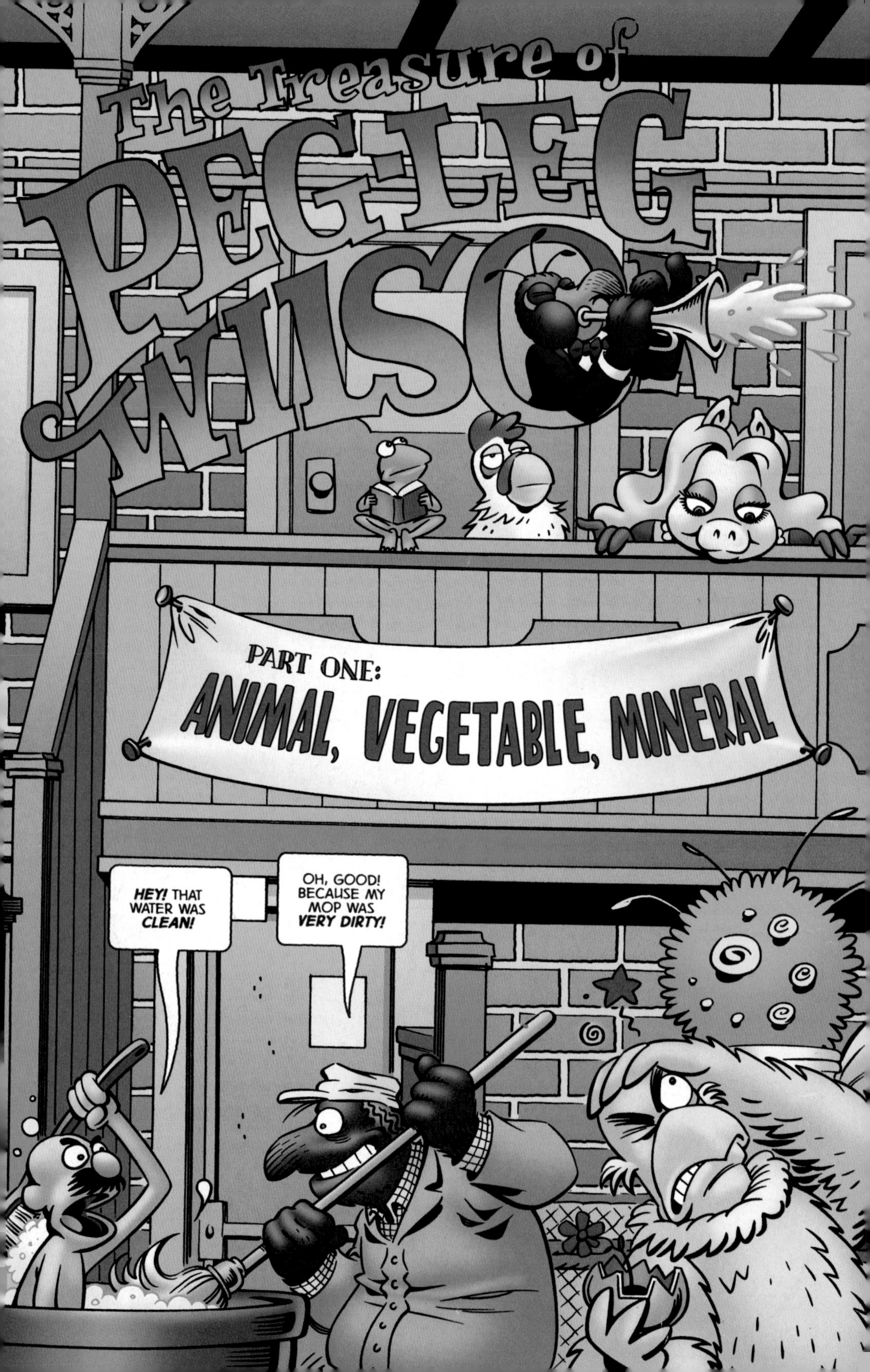
The Treasure of
PEGLEG WILSON
PART ONE:
ANIMAL, VEGETABLE, MINERAL
HEY! THAT WATER WAS CLEAN!
OH, GOOD! BECAUSE MY MOP WAS VERY DIRTY!

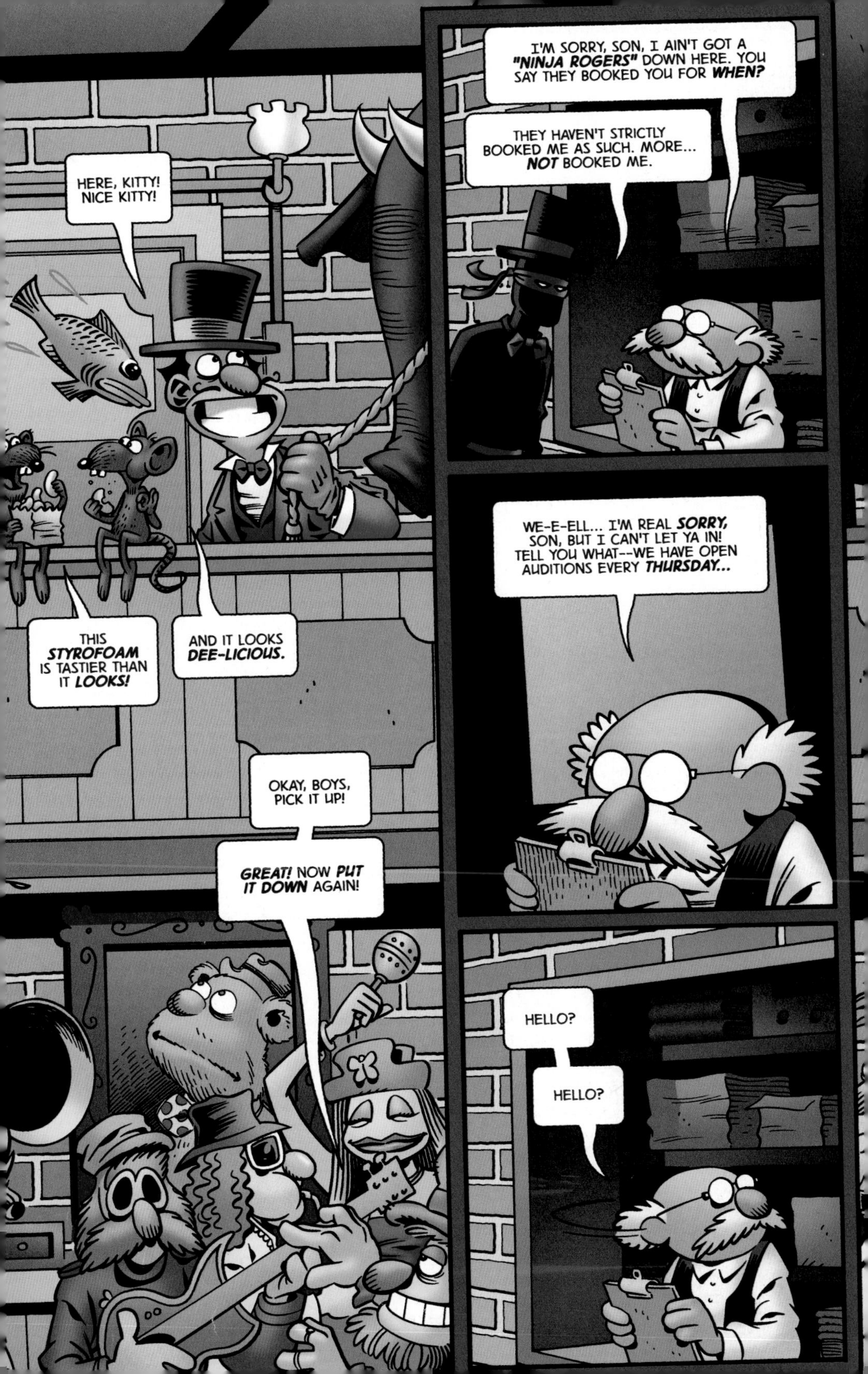
HERE, KITTY! NICE KITTY!
THIS STYROFOAM IS TASTIER THAN IT LOOKS!
AND IT LOOKS DEE-LICIOUS.
OKAY, BOYS, PICK IT UP!
GREAT! NOW PUT IT DOWN AGAIN!
I'M SORRY, SON, I AIN'T GOT A "NINJA ROGERS" DOWN HERE. YOU SAY THEY BOOKED YOU FOR WHEN?
THEY HAVEN'T STRICTLY BOOKED ME AS SUCH. MORE... NOT BOOKED ME.
WE-E-ELL... I'M REAL SORRY, SON, BUT I CAN'T LET YA IN! TELL YOU WHAT--WE HAVE OPEN AUDITIONS EVERY THURSDAY...
HELLO?
HELLO?

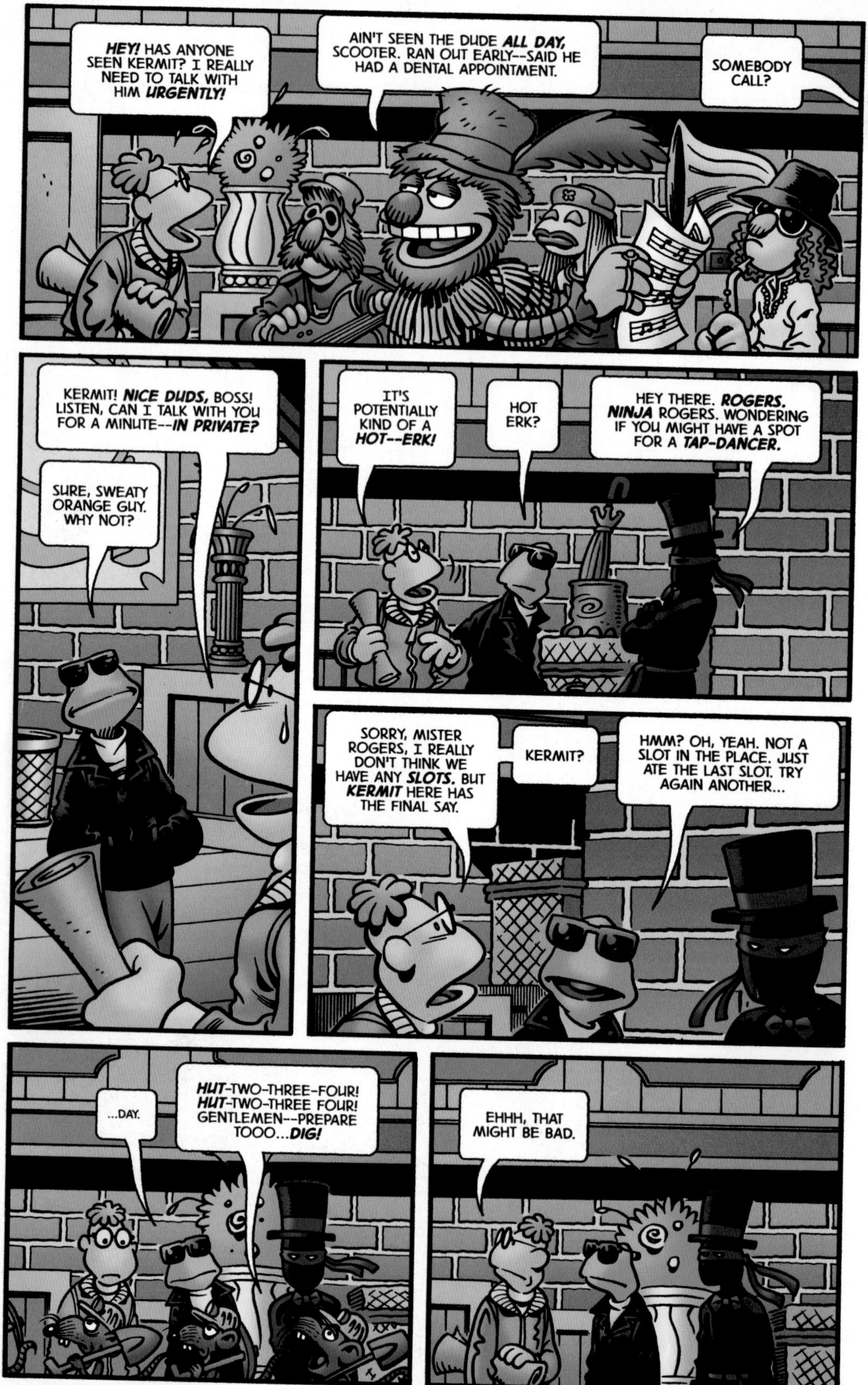
HEY! HAS ANYONE SEEN KERMIT? I REALLY NEED TO TALK WITH HIM URGENTLY!
AIN'T SEEN THE DUDE ALL DAY, SCOOTER. RAN OUT EARLY--SAID HE HAD A DENTAL APPOINTMENT.
SOMEBODY CALL?
KERMIT! NICE DUDS, BOSS! LISTEN, CAN I TALK WITH YOU FOR A MINUTE--IN PRIVATE?
SURE, SWEATY ORANGE GUY. WHY NOT?
IT'S POTENTIALLY KIND OF A HOT--ERK!
HOT ERK?
HEY THERE. ROGERS. NINJA ROGERS. WONDERING IF YOU MIGHT HAVE A SPOT FOR A TAP-DANCER.
SORRY, MISTER ROGERS, I REALLY DON'T THINK WE HAVE ANY SLOTS. BUT KERMIT HERE HAS THE FINAL SAY.
KERMIT?
HMM? OH, YEAH. NOT A SLOT IN THE PLACE. JUST ATE THE LAST SLOT. TRY AGAIN ANOTHER...
...DAY.
HUT-TWO-THREE-FOUR! HUT-TWO-THREE FOUR! GENTLEMEN--PREPARE TOOO...DIG!
EHHH, THAT MIGHT BE BAD.

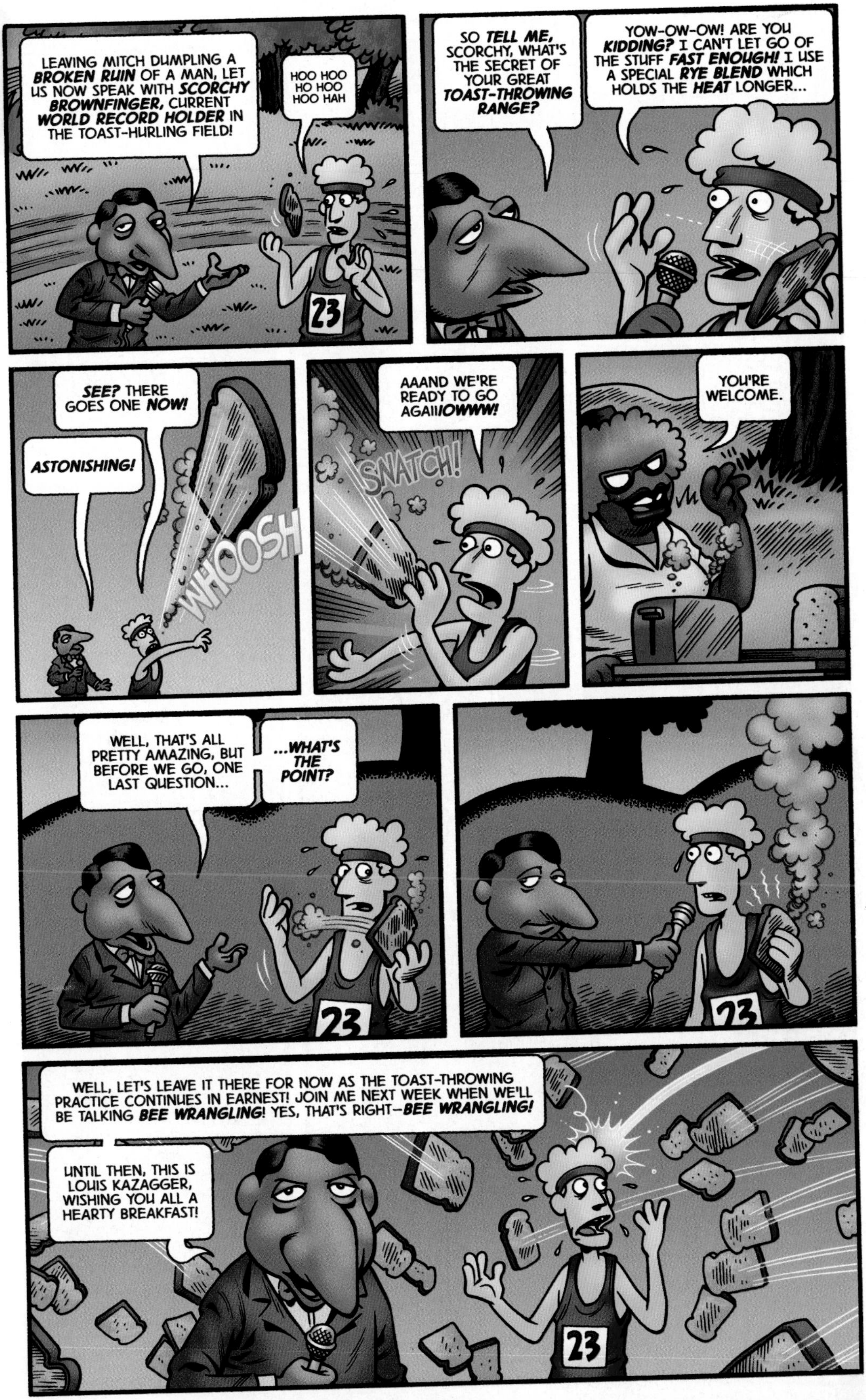
LEAVING MITCH DUMPLING A **BROKEN RUIN** OF A MAN, LET US NOW SPEAK WITH **SCORCHY BROWNFINGER,** CURRENT **WORLD RECORD HOLDER** IN THE TOAST-HURLING FIELD!
HOO HOO HO HOO HOO HAH
SO **TELL ME,** SCORCHY, WHAT'S THE SECRET OF YOUR GREAT **TOAST-THROWING RANGE?**
YOW-OW-OW! ARE YOU **KIDDING?** I CAN'T LET GO OF THE STUFF **FAST ENOUGH!** I USE A SPECIAL **RYE BLEND** WHICH HOLDS THE **HEAT** LONGER...
SEE? THERE GOES ONE **NOW!**
ASTONISHING!
WHOOSH
AAAND WE'RE READY TO GO AGAII**OWWW!**
SNATCH!
YOU'RE WELCOME.
WELL, THAT'S ALL PRETTY AMAZING, BUT BEFORE WE GO, ONE LAST QUESTION...
...WHAT'S THE POINT?
23
WELL, LET'S LEAVE IT THERE FOR NOW AS THE TOAST-THROWING PRACTICE CONTINUES IN EARNEST! JOIN ME NEXT WEEK WHEN WE'LL BE TALKING **BEE WRANGLING**! YES, THAT'S RIGHT–**BEE WRANGLING!**
UNTIL THEN, THIS IS LOUIS KAZAGGER, WISHING YOU ALL A HEARTY BREAKFAST!

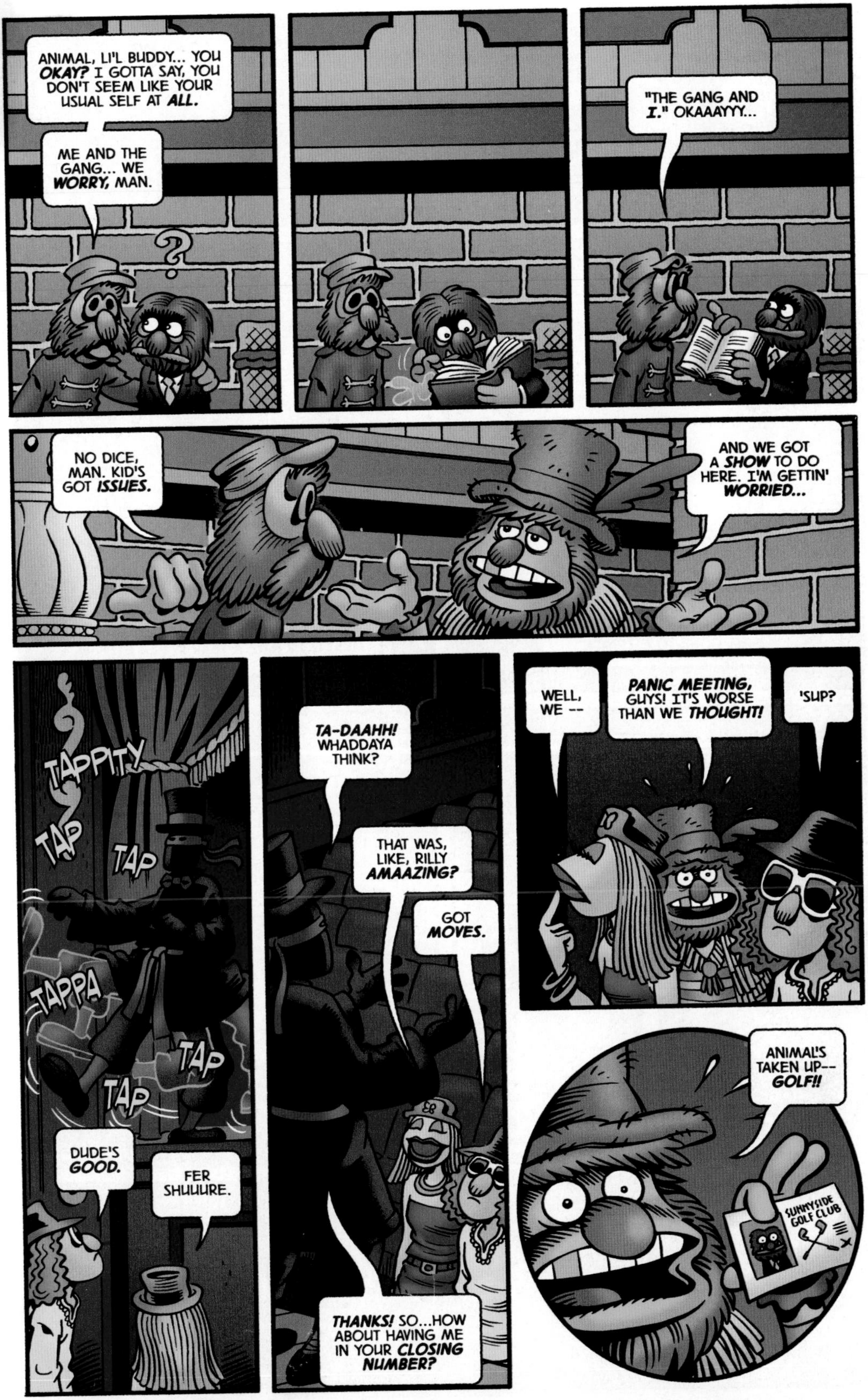

ANIMAL, LI'L BUDDY... YOU OKAY? I GOTTA SAY, YOU DON'T SEEM LIKE YOUR USUAL SELF AT ALL.
ME AND THE GANG... WE WORRY, MAN.
?
"THE GANG AND I." OKAAAYYY...
NO DICE, MAN. KID'S GOT ISSUES.
AND WE GOT A SHOW TO DO HERE. I'M GETTIN' WORRIED...
TAPPITY
TAP
TAP
TAPPA
TAP
TAP
DUDE'S GOOD.
FER SHUUURE.
TA-DAAHH! WHADDAYA THINK?
THAT WAS, LIKE, RILLY AMAAZING?
GOT MOVES.
THANKS! SO...HOW ABOUT HAVING ME IN YOUR CLOSING NUMBER?
WELL, WE --
PANIC MEETING, GUYS! IT'S WORSE THAN WE THOUGHT!
'SUP?
ANIMAL'S TAKEN UP-- GOLF!!
SUNNYSIDE GOLF CLUB

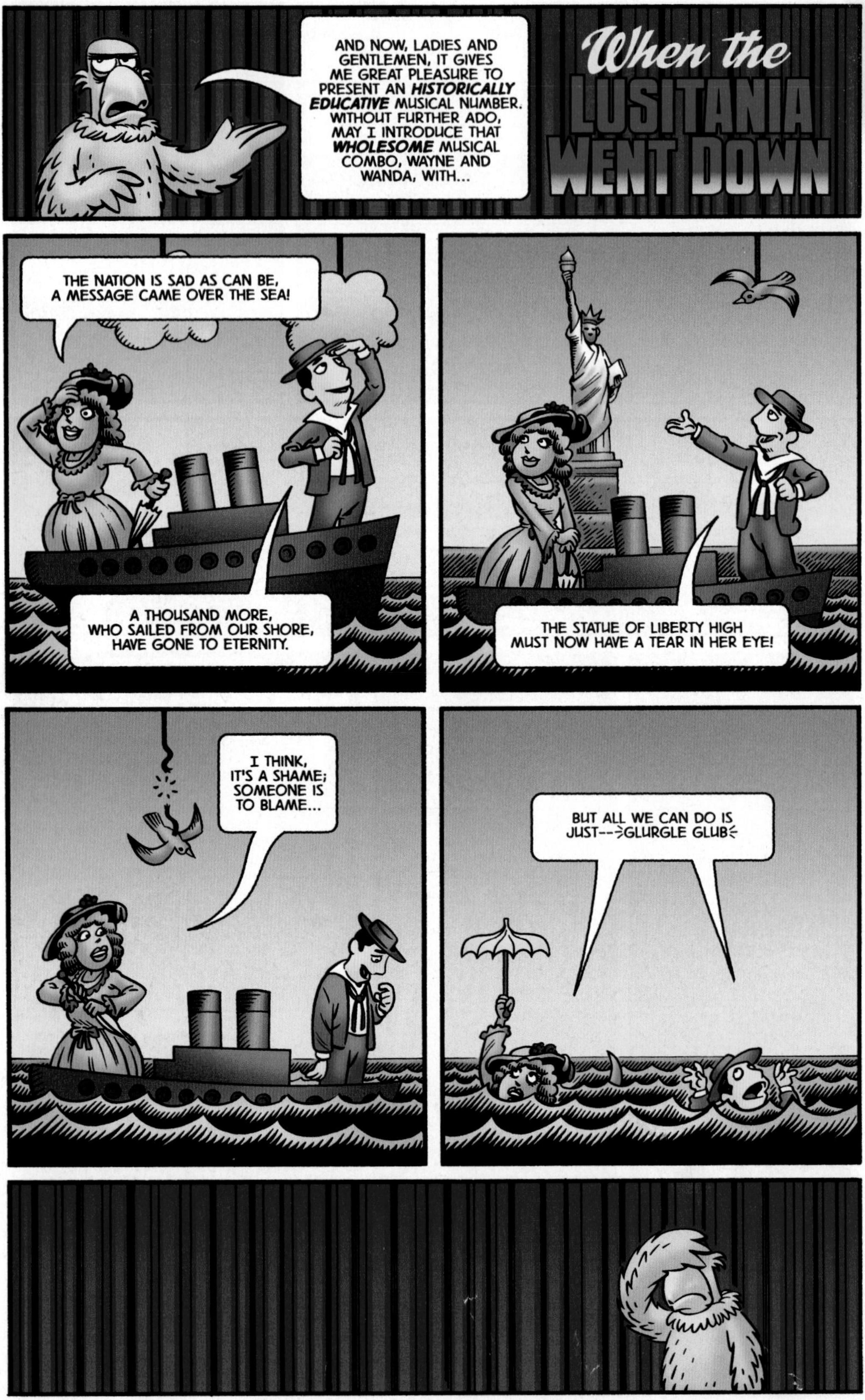
AND NOW, LADIES AND GENTLEMEN, IT GIVES ME GREAT PLEASURE TO PRESENT AN HISTORICALLY EDUCATIVE MUSICAL NUMBER. WITHOUT FURTHER ADO, MAY I INTRODUCE THAT WHOLESOME MUSICAL COMBO, WAYNE AND WANDA, WITH...
When the LUSITANIA WENT DOWN
THE NATION IS SAD AS CAN BE, A MESSAGE CAME OVER THE SEA!
A THOUSAND MORE, WHO SAILED FROM OUR SHORE, HAVE GONE TO ETERNITY.
THE STATUE OF LIBERTY HIGH MUST NOW HAVE A TEAR IN HER EYE!
I THINK, IT'S A SHAME; SOMEONE IS TO BLAME...
BUT ALL WE CAN DO IS JUST--GLURGLE GLUB

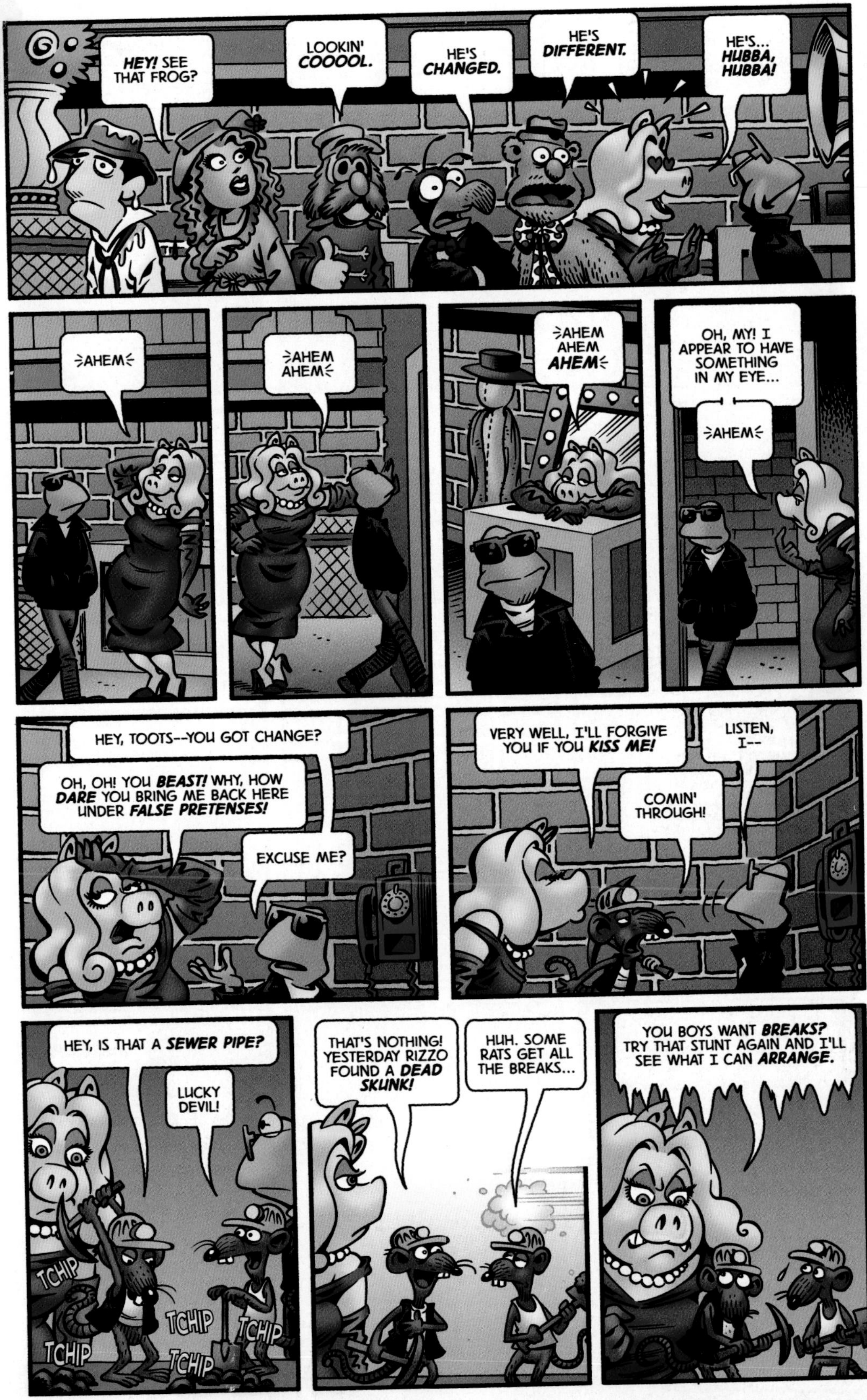

HEY! SEE THAT FROG?
LOOKIN' COOOOL.
HE'S CHANGED.
HE'S DIFFERENT.
HE'S... HUBBA, HUBBA!
AHEM
AHEM AHEM
AHEM AHEM AHEM
OH, MY! I APPEAR TO HAVE SOMETHING IN MY EYE...
AHEM
HEY, TOOTS--YOU GOT CHANGE?
OH, OH! YOU BEAST! WHY, HOW DARE YOU BRING ME BACK HERE UNDER FALSE PRETENSES!
EXCUSE ME?
VERY WELL, I'LL FORGIVE YOU IF YOU KISS ME!
LISTEN, I--
COMIN' THROUGH!
HEY, IS THAT A SEWER PIPE?
LUCKY DEVIL!
TCHIP
TCHIP
TCHIP
TCHIP
TCHIP
THAT'S NOTHING! YESTERDAY RIZZO FOUND A DEAD SKUNK!
HUH. SOME RATS GET ALL THE BREAKS...
YOU BOYS WANT BREAKS? TRY THAT STUNT AGAIN AND I'LL SEE WHAT I CAN ARRANGE.

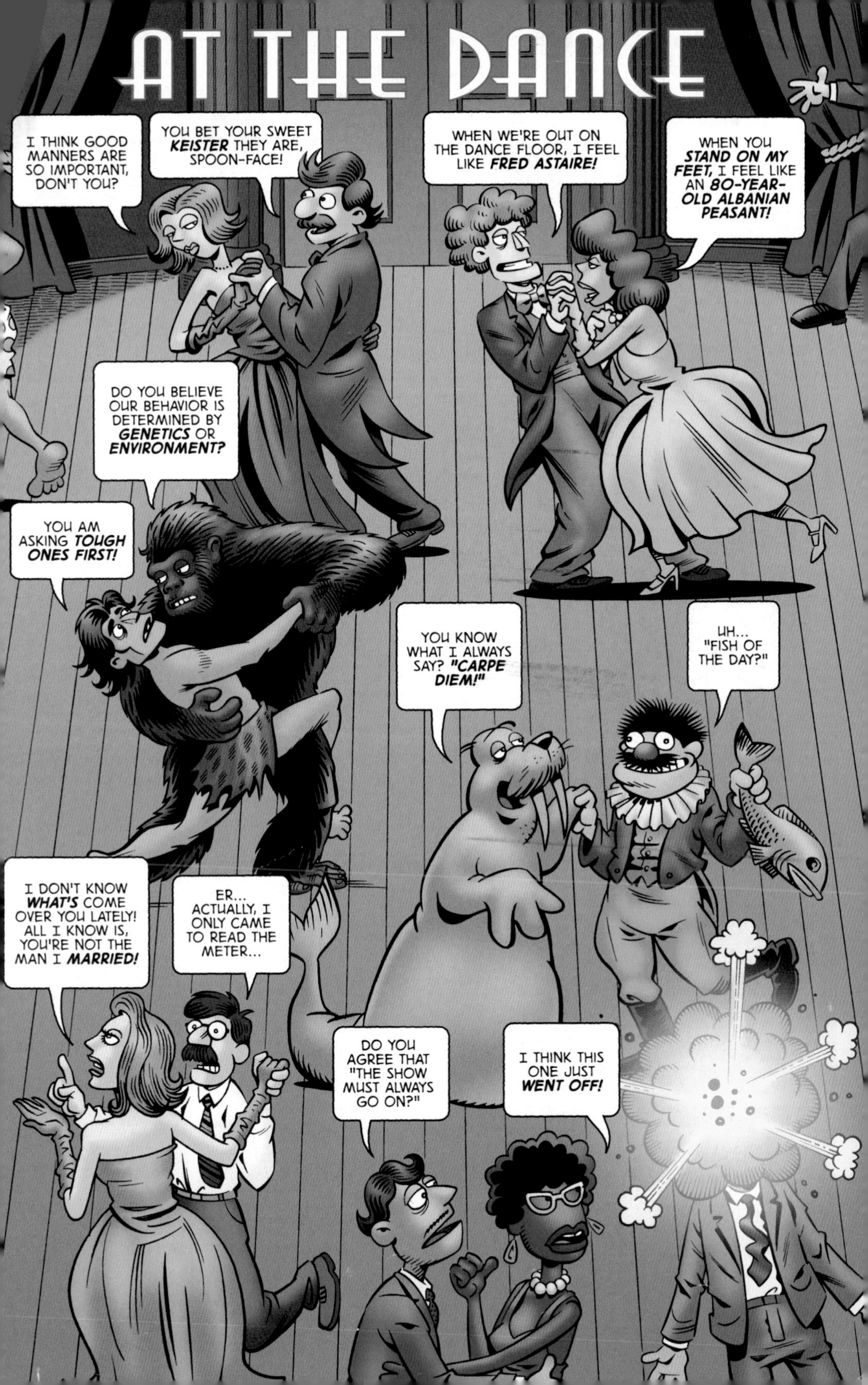
AT THE DANCE
I THINK GOOD MANNERS ARE SO IMPORTANT, DON'T YOU?
YOU BET YOUR SWEET KEISTER THEY ARE, SPOON-FACE!
WHEN WE'RE OUT ON THE DANCE FLOOR, I FEEL LIKE FRED ASTAIRE!
WHEN YOU STAND ON MY FEET, I FEEL LIKE AN 80-YEAR-OLD ALBANIAN PEASANT!
DO YOU BELIEVE OUR BEHAVIOR IS DETERMINED BY GENETICS OR ENVIRONMENT?
YOU AM ASKING TOUGH ONES FIRST!
YOU KNOW WHAT I ALWAYS SAY? "CARPE DIEM!"
UH... "FISH OF THE DAY?"
I DON'T KNOW WHAT'S COME OVER YOU LATELY! ALL I KNOW IS, YOU'RE NOT THE MAN I MARRIED!
ER... ACTUALLY, I ONLY CAME TO READ THE METER...
DO YOU AGREE THAT "THE SHOW MUST ALWAYS GO ON?"
I THINK THIS ONE JUST WENT OFF!

AND NOW...

For your Delight and Delectation

The One... The Only...

FOZZIE BEAR

As seen at the Sunny Days Retirement Home and on "Late Night with Ernst Strains"

AAAH! GOOD EVENING, LADIES AND GERMS! HEY, DID YOU HEAR THE ONE ABOUT THE GORILLA WITH NO EARS? *NEITHER DID HE!*

B'DUM-TSS!

I'M HERE ALL WEEK.

SO THERE WAS THIS *ZEBRA*, AND HE KEPT GETTING *RUN OVER* ON *CROSSINGS,* AND HE DECIDED THIS WAS SOMETHING HE WASN'T GOING TO PUT UP WITH. SO--

EH?

YEAH, I *KNOW* I ENDED A SENTENCE WITH A PREPOSITION. DO YOU HAVE ANY IDEA HOW AWKWARD THAT WOULD--

SIGH OH, ALL RIGHT...

SO HE DECIDED THIS WAS A THING UP WITH WHICH HE WOULD NOT PUT.

AND, UH...

I'VE LOST MY PLACE NOW.

ANIMAL! YOU'VE MESSED UP MY ACT!

THAT'S RIGHT! *BLAME THE DRUMMER!*

"OH, MY ACT ISN'T FUNNY BECAUSE I DON'T HAVE A FRENCH HORN SOLO!" HO HO HO!

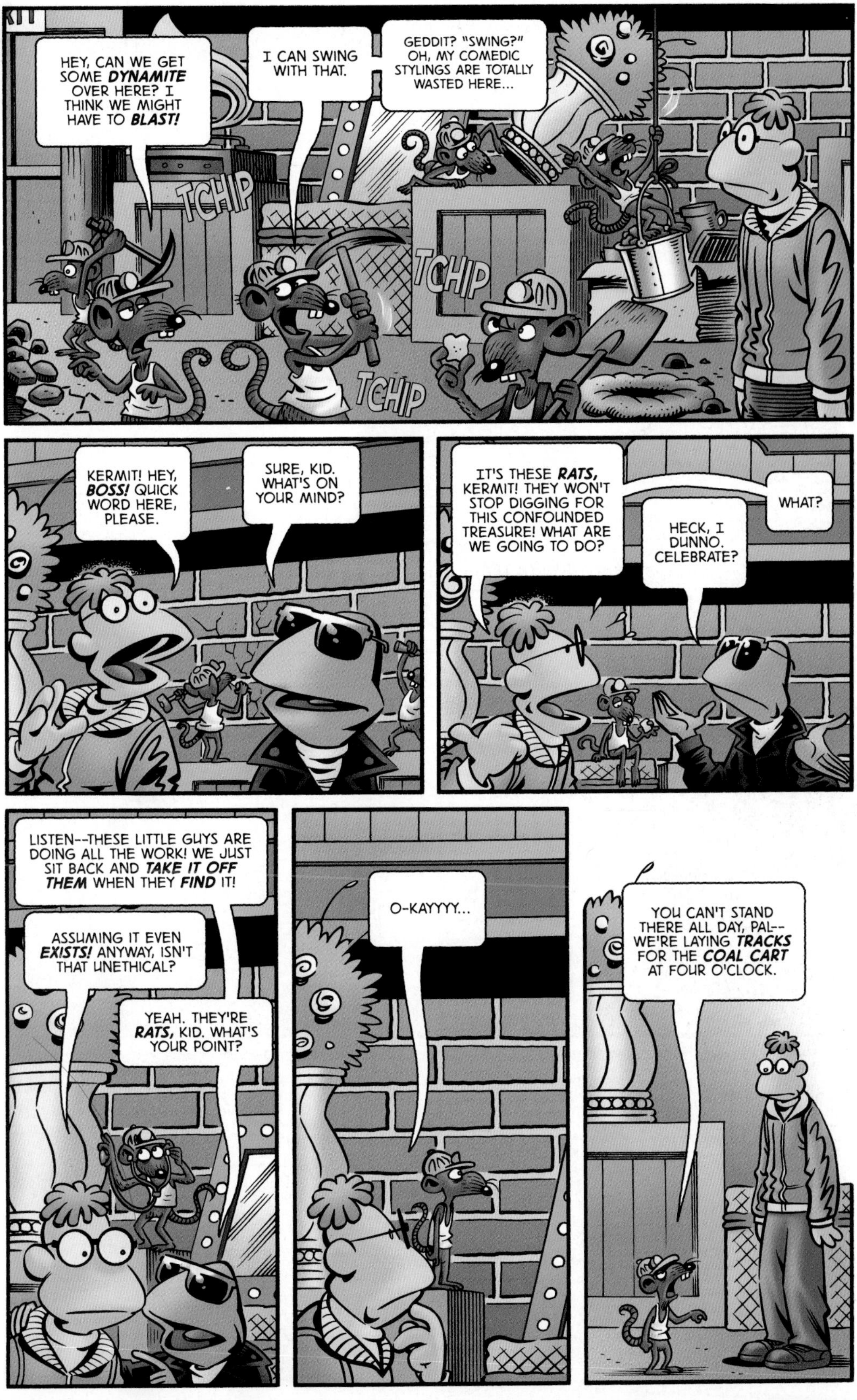
HEY, CAN WE GET SOME **DYNAMITE** OVER HERE? I THINK WE MIGHT HAVE TO **BLAST!**
I CAN SWING WITH THAT.
GEDDIT? "SWING?" OH, MY COMEDIC STYLINGS ARE TOTALLY WASTED HERE...
TCHIP
TCHIP
TCHIP
KERMIT! HEY, **BOSS!** QUICK WORD HERE, PLEASE.
SURE, KID. WHAT'S ON YOUR MIND?
IT'S THESE **RATS,** KERMIT! THEY WON'T STOP DIGGING FOR THIS CONFOUNDED TREASURE! WHAT ARE WE GOING TO DO?
HECK, I DUNNO. CELEBRATE?
WHAT?
LISTEN--THESE LITTLE GUYS ARE DOING ALL THE WORK! WE JUST SIT BACK AND **TAKE IT OFF THEM** WHEN THEY **FIND** IT!
ASSUMING IT EVEN **EXISTS!** ANYWAY, ISN'T THAT UNETHICAL?
YEAH. THEY'RE **RATS,** KID. WHAT'S YOUR POINT?
O-KAYYYY...
YOU CAN'T STAND THERE ALL DAY, PAL--WE'RE LAYING **TRACKS** FOR THE **COAL CART** AT FOUR O'CLOCK.

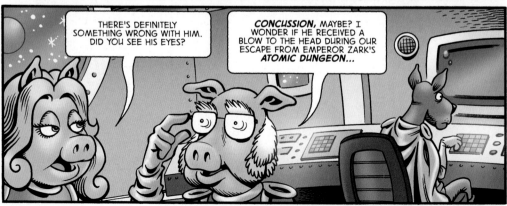

HAY FEVER! I BET THAT'S IT! HE GETS THAT *EVERY* SPRING!

WILDLY IMPROBABLE, PIGGY. THE SHIP IS *CLIMATE-CONTROLLED.* WE'RE *SIX LIGHT-YEARS AWAY* FROM THE NEAREST *SPECK* OF POLLEN!

TAKE OFF THAT *RIDICULOUS* HALLOWEEN COSTUME AND MAKE YOUR REPORT, HOGTHROB!!

CALL ME CRAZY...BUT I THINK THE TELEPORTER TURNED HIM INTO A KANGAROO.

TWO WORDS, HOGTHROB... *COURT-MARTIAL!*

A *KANGAROO?* WHY, THAT'S... THAT'S...

UM.

YEAH, I KNOW! BUT *LOOK* AT THE GUY! WE NEED TO GET HIM BACK IN THAT TELEPORTER SO WE CAN *REVERSE THE PROCESS!*

HUM DE DUM...OH, THAT FEELS *SO* MUCH BETTER.

÷GNNNN÷ *SHOVE,* PIGGY! HE GOT *OUT,* HE CAN DARN WELL *GET IN!*

I'M SHOVING, I'M *SHOVING!* HE'S PUT ON A *POUND OR TWELVE,* I'M TELLING YA!

I AM FORCED TO CONCLUDE THAT YOUR SHIP HAS BEEN *TAKEN OVER!* IN FIVE MINUTES WE WILL *BLAST YOU OUT OF THE SKY!*

OH, YES... IT'S GOOD TO KNOW I CAN TAKE A SHOWER AND LEAVE THE SHIP IN SAFE HANDS.

I WONDER WHAT'S ON CHANNEL ZERO LATER TONIGHT...?

SUB-ETHER WAVEBAND Guide

WILL THE GALACTIC COUCIL REDUCE THE SWINETREK TO ATOMS?

WILL MISS PIGGY AND DOCTOR STRANGEPORK TELEPORT THE KANGAROO ANYWHERE NICE FOR HIS SUMMER VACATION?

WILL LINK HOGTHROB WATCH "PIRANHA CHALLENGE" OR "WORLD OF CAKES"?. TUNE IN NEXT TIME AND STARE POINTLESSLY AT THE CLOUD OF FLOATING SPACE DUST THAT USED TO BE...

PIGS IN SRAAACE!

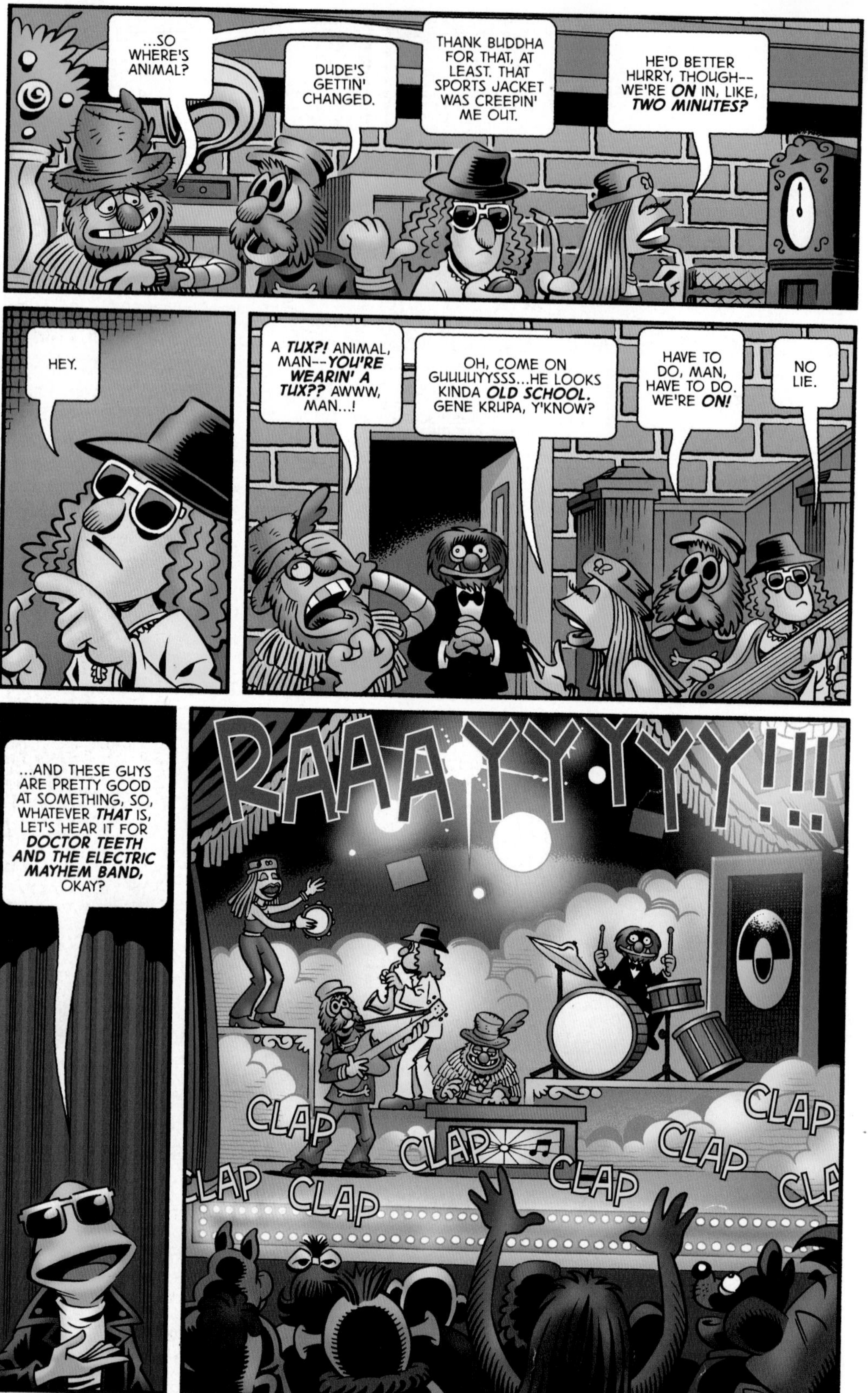
...SO WHERE'S ANIMAL?
DUDE'S GETTIN' CHANGED.
THANK BUDDHA FOR THAT, AT LEAST. THAT SPORTS JACKET WAS CREEPIN' ME OUT.
HE'D BETTER HURRY, THOUGH-- WE'RE *ON* IN, LIKE, *TWO MINUTES?*
HEY.
A *TUX?!* ANIMAL, MAN--*YOU'RE WEARIN' A TUX??* AWWW, MAN...!
OH, COME ON GUUUUYYSSS...HE LOOKS KINDA *OLD SCHOOL.* GENE KRUPA, Y'KNOW?
HAVE TO DO, MAN, HAVE TO DO. WE'RE *ON!*
NO LIE.
...AND THESE GUYS ARE PRETTY GOOD AT SOMETHING, SO, WHATEVER *THAT* IS, LET'S HEAR IT FOR *DOCTOR TEETH AND THE ELECTRIC MAYHEM BAND,* OKAY?
RAAAYYYYY!!!
CLAP CLAP CLAP CLAP CLAP CLAP CLAP CLAP

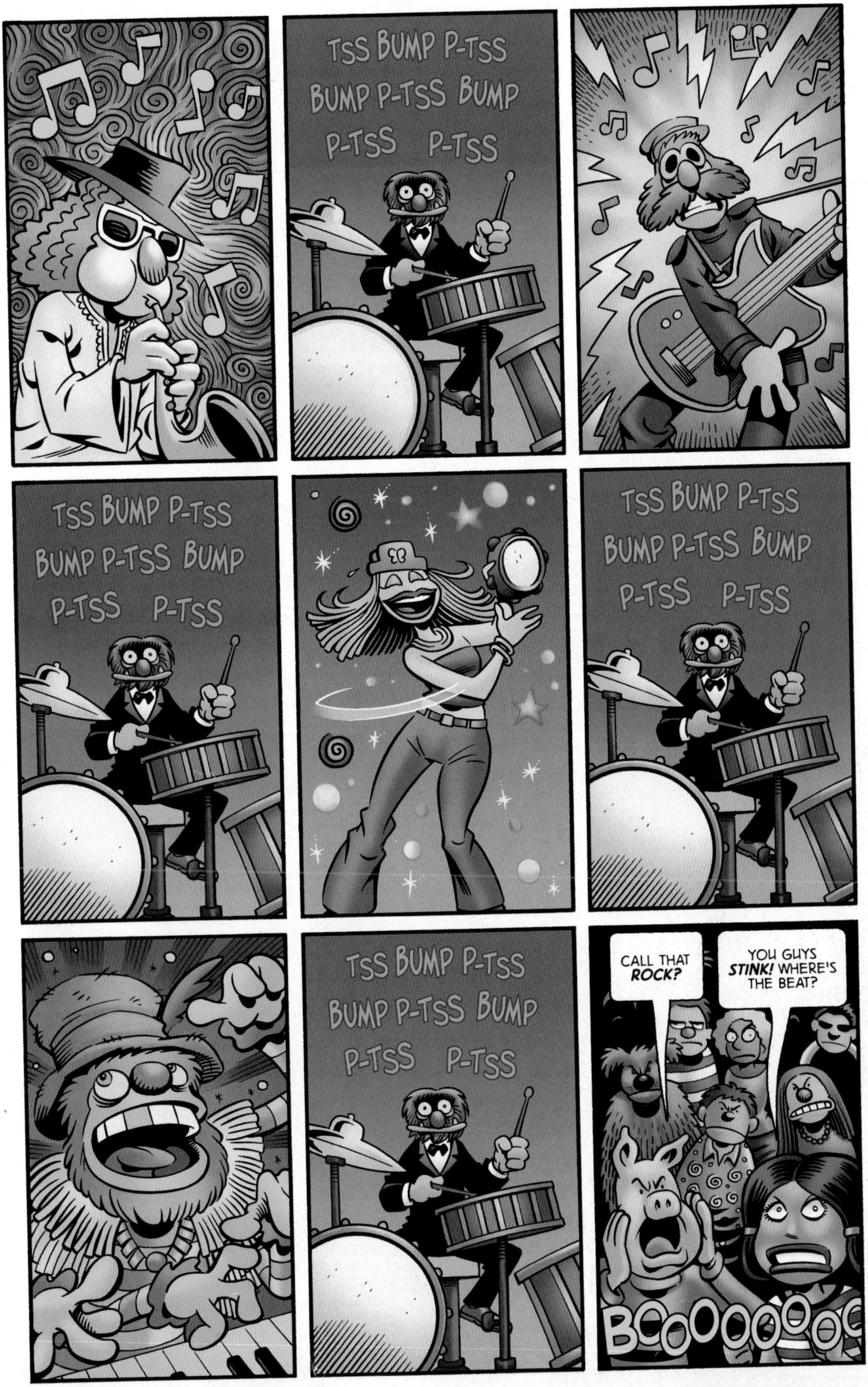

TSS BUMP P-TSS
BUMP P-TSS BUMP
P-TSS P-TSS
TSS BUMP P-TSS
BUMP P-TSS BUMP
P-TSS P-TSS
TSS BUMP P-TSS
BUMP P-TSS BUMP
P-TSS P-TSS
TSS BUMP P-TSS
BUMP P-TSS BUMP
P-TSS P-TSS
CALL THAT ROCK?
YOU GUYS STINK! WHERE'S THE BEAT?
BOOOOOOOO

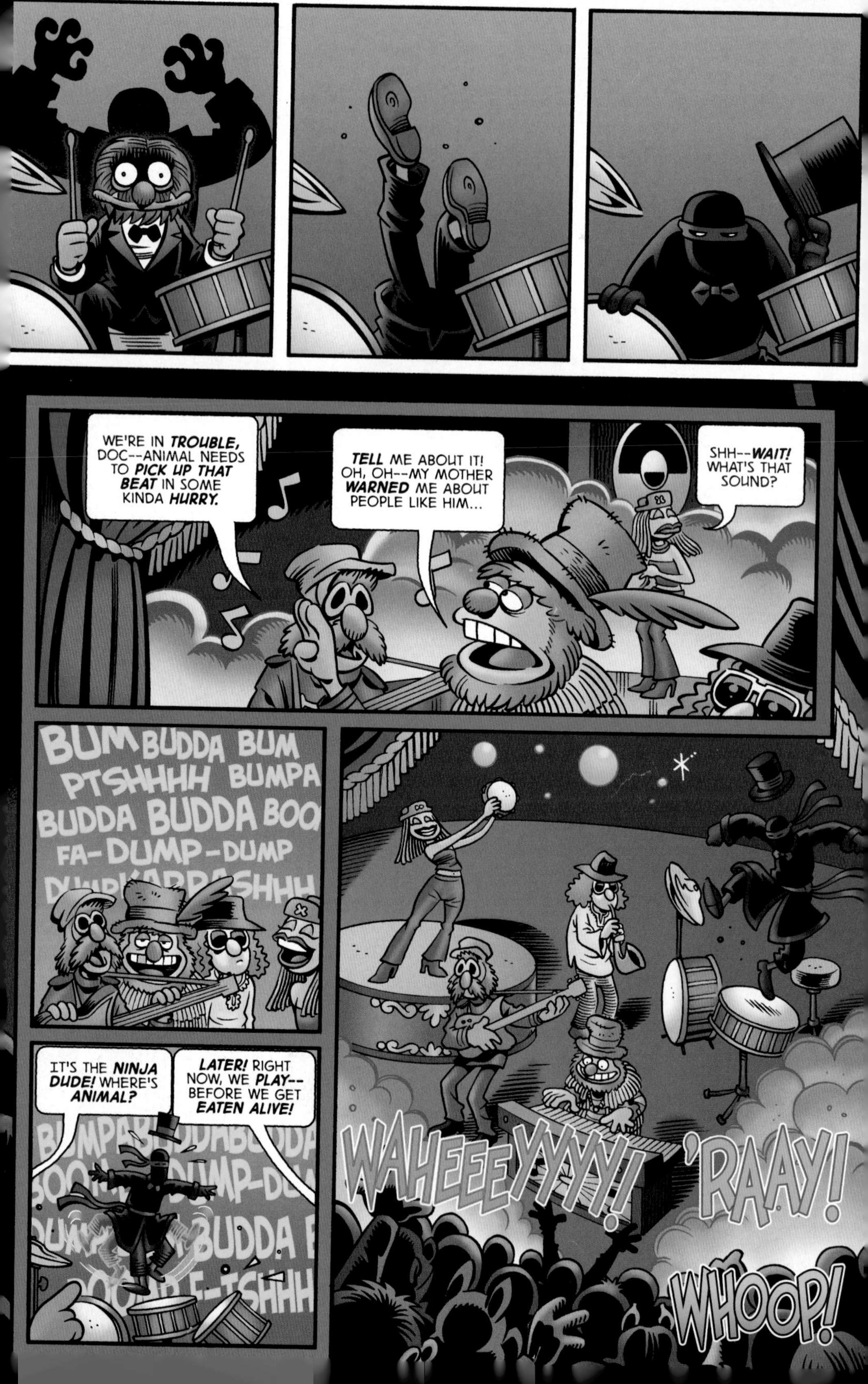
WE'RE IN **TROUBLE,** DOC--ANIMAL NEEDS TO **PICK UP THAT BEAT** IN SOME KINDA **HURRY.**
TELL ME ABOUT IT! OH, OH--MY MOTHER **WARNED** ME ABOUT PEOPLE LIKE HIM...
SHH--**WAIT!** WHAT'S THAT SOUND?
BUM BUDDA BUM
PTSHHHH BUMPA
BUDDA BUDDA
FA-DUMP-DUMP
IT'S THE **NINJA DUDE!** WHERE'S **ANIMAL?**
LATER! RIGHT NOW, WE **PLAY--** BEFORE WE GET **EATEN ALIVE!**
WAHEEEYYYY!
'RAAY!
WHOOP!

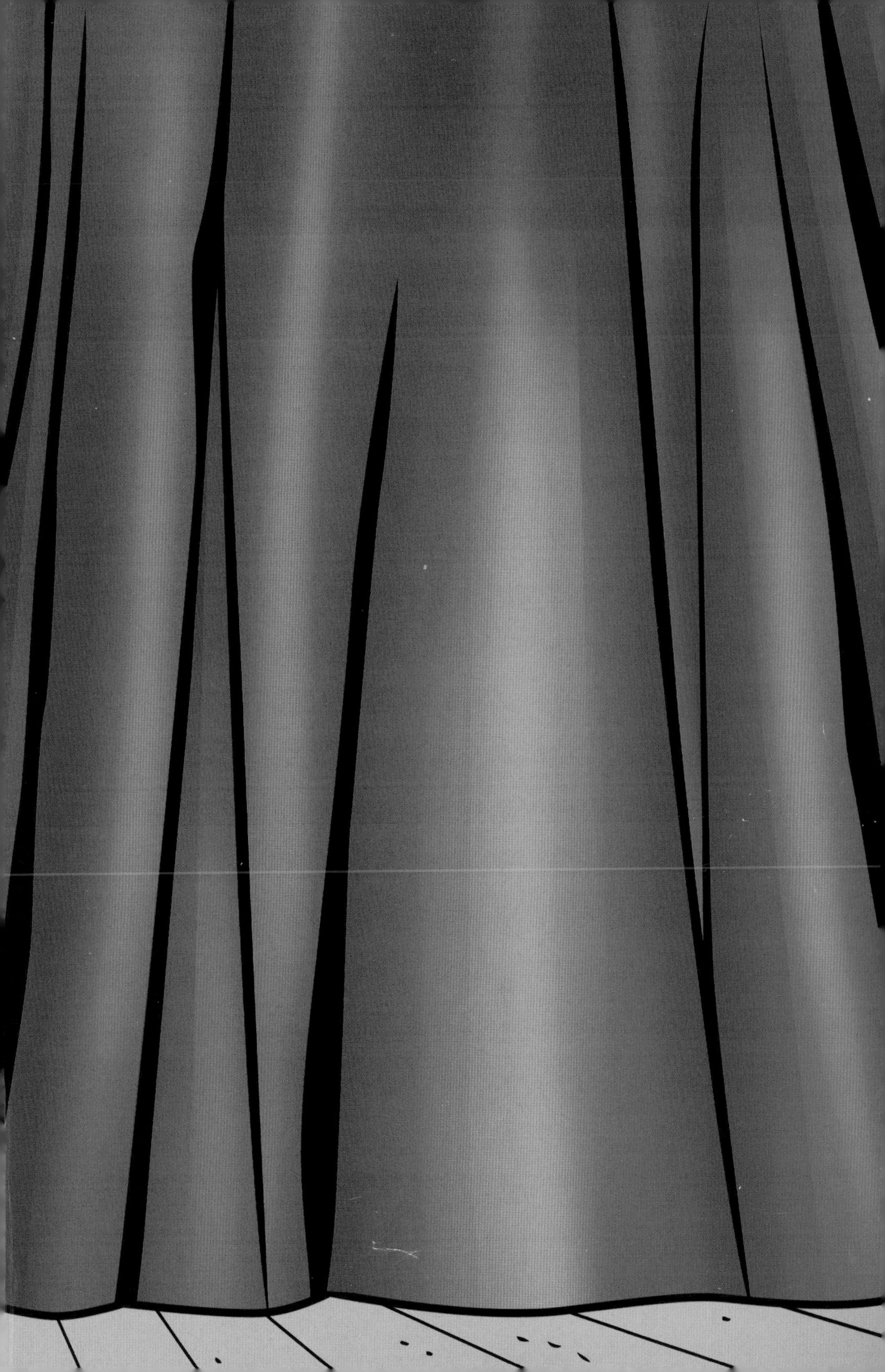

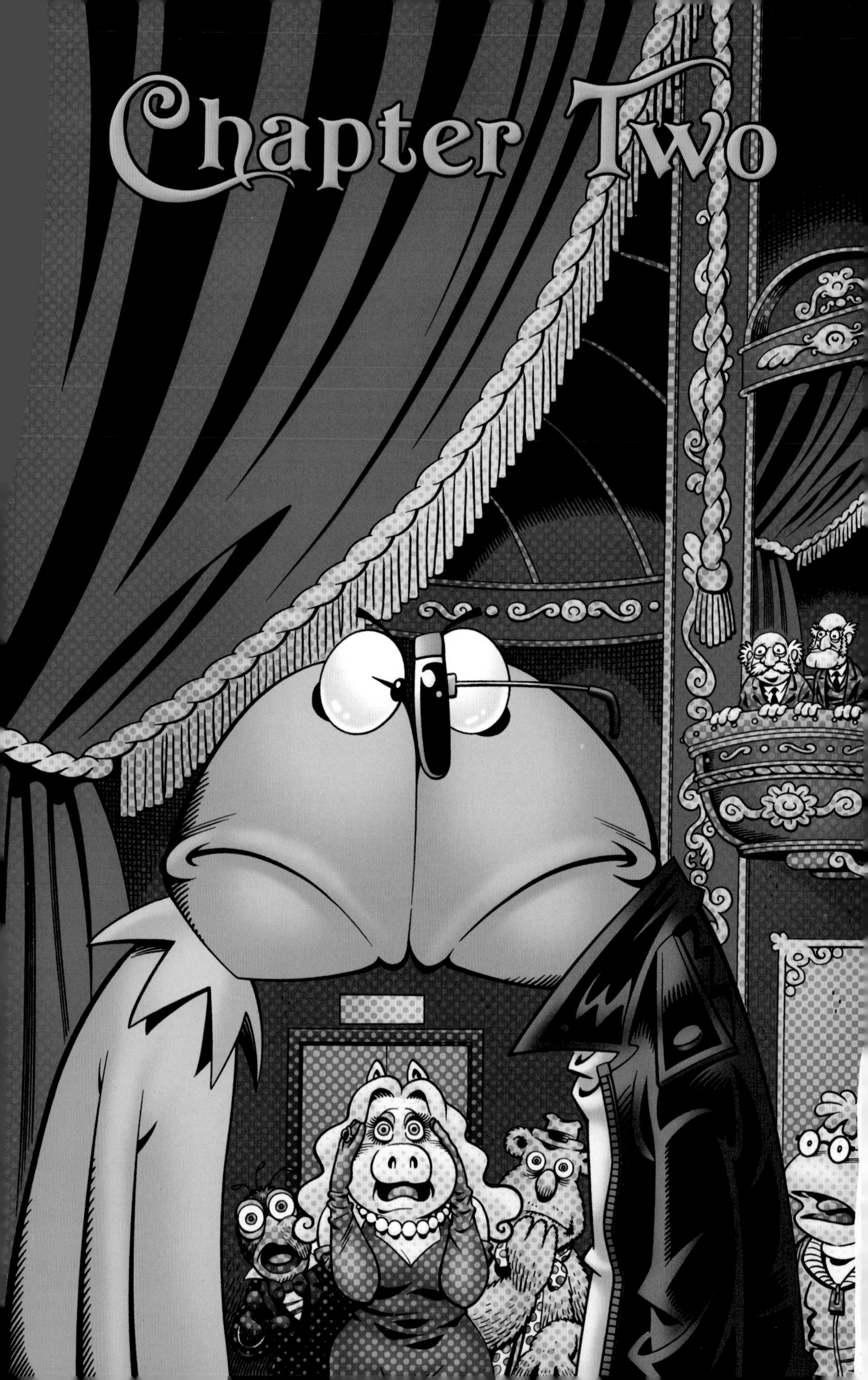
Chapter Two

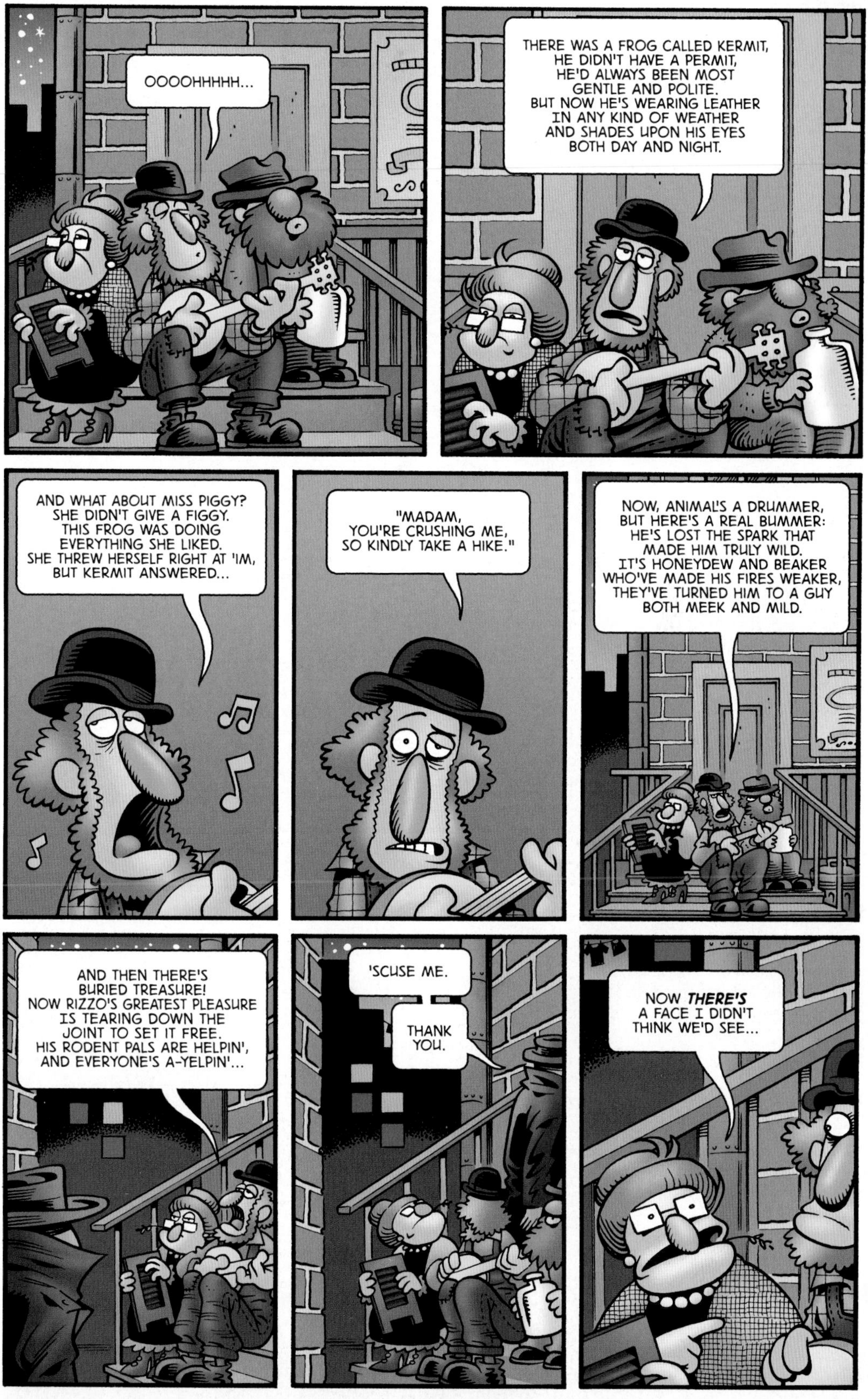
OOOOHHHHH...
THERE WAS A FROG CALLED KERMIT, HE DIDN'T HAVE A PERMIT, HE'D ALWAYS BEEN MOST GENTLE AND POLITE. BUT NOW HE'S WEARING LEATHER IN ANY KIND OF WEATHER AND SHADES UPON HIS EYES BOTH DAY AND NIGHT.
AND WHAT ABOUT MISS PIGGY? SHE DIDN'T GIVE A FIGGY. THIS FROG WAS DOING EVERYTHING SHE LIKED. SHE THREW HERSELF RIGHT AT 'IM, BUT KERMIT ANSWERED...
"MADAM, YOU'RE CRUSHING ME, SO KINDLY TAKE A HIKE."
NOW, ANIMAL'S A DRUMMER, BUT HERE'S A REAL BUMMER: HE'S LOST THE SPARK THAT MADE HIM TRULY WILD. IT'S HONEYDEW AND BEAKER WHO'VE MADE HIS FIRES WEAKER, THEY'VE TURNED HIM TO A GUY BOTH MEEK AND MILD.
AND THEN THERE'S BURIED TREASURE! NOW RIZZO'S GREATEST PLEASURE IS TEARING DOWN THE JOINT TO SET IT FREE. HIS RODENT PALS ARE HELPIN', AND EVERYONE'S A-YELPIN'...
'SCUSE ME.
THANK YOU.
NOW ***THERE'S*** A FACE I DIDN'T THINK WE'D SEE...

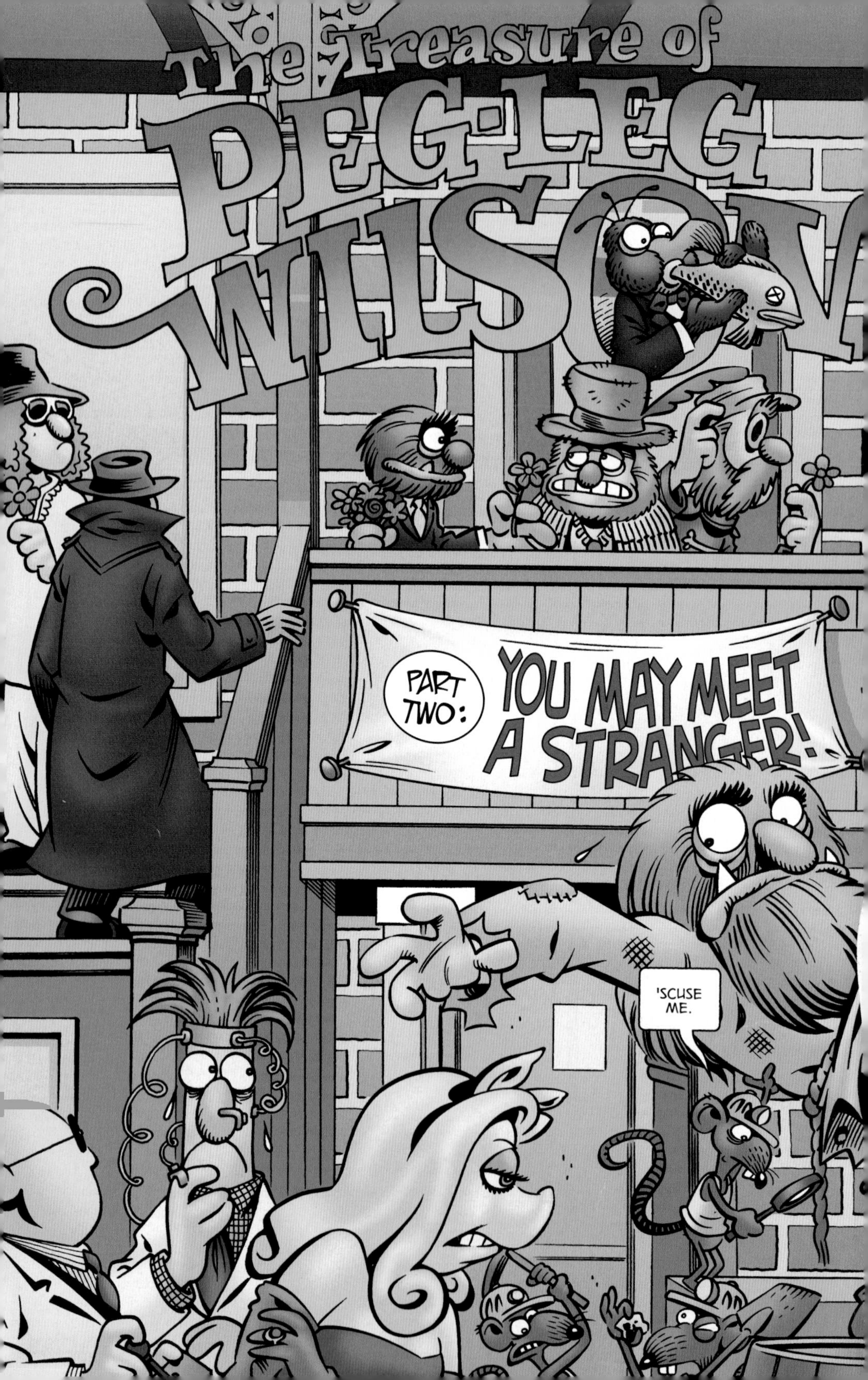
The Treasure of
PEG-LEG WILSON
PART TWO: YOU MAY MEET A STRANGER!
'SCUSE ME.

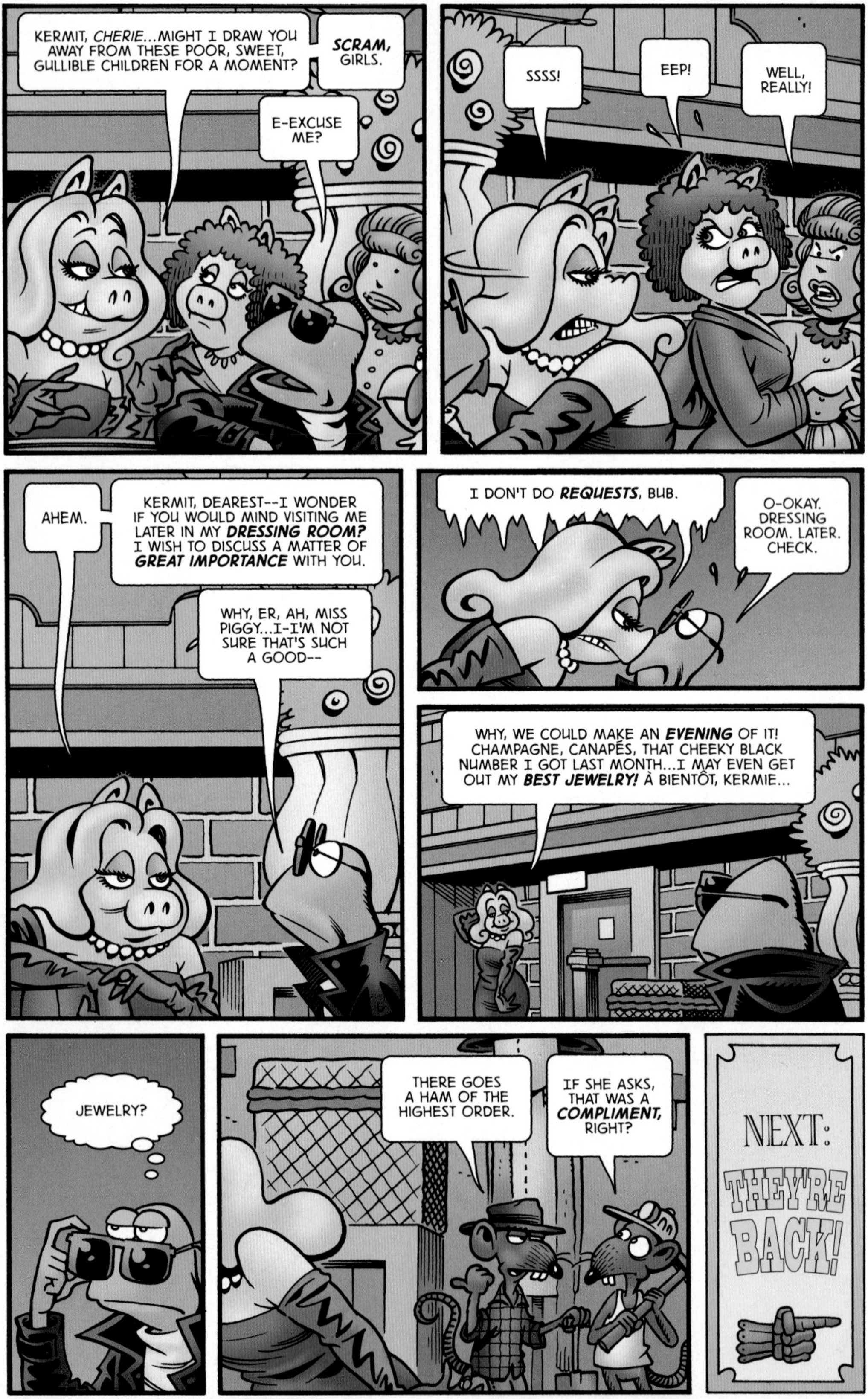

KERMIT, *CHERIE*...MIGHT I DRAW YOU AWAY FROM THESE POOR, SWEET, GULLIBLE CHILDREN FOR A MOMENT?
SCRAM, GIRLS.
E-EXCUSE ME?
SSSS!
EEP!
WELL, REALLY!
AHEM.
KERMIT, DEAREST--I WONDER IF YOU WOULD MIND VISITING ME LATER IN MY ***DRESSING ROOM?*** I WISH TO DISCUSS A MATTER OF ***GREAT IMPORTANCE*** WITH YOU.
WHY, ER, AH, MISS PIGGY...I-I'M NOT SURE THAT'S SUCH A GOOD--
I DON'T DO ***REQUESTS***, BUB.
O-OKAY. DRESSING ROOM. LATER. CHECK.
WHY, WE COULD MAKE AN ***EVENING*** OF IT! CHAMPAGNE, CANAPÉS, THAT CHEEKY BLACK NUMBER I GOT LAST MONTH...I MAY EVEN GET OUT MY ***BEST JEWELRY!*** À BIENTÔT, KERMIE...
JEWELRY?
THERE GOES A HAM OF THE HIGHEST ORDER.
IF SHE ASKS, THAT WAS A ***COMPLIMENT,*** RIGHT?
NEXT:
THEY'RE BACK!

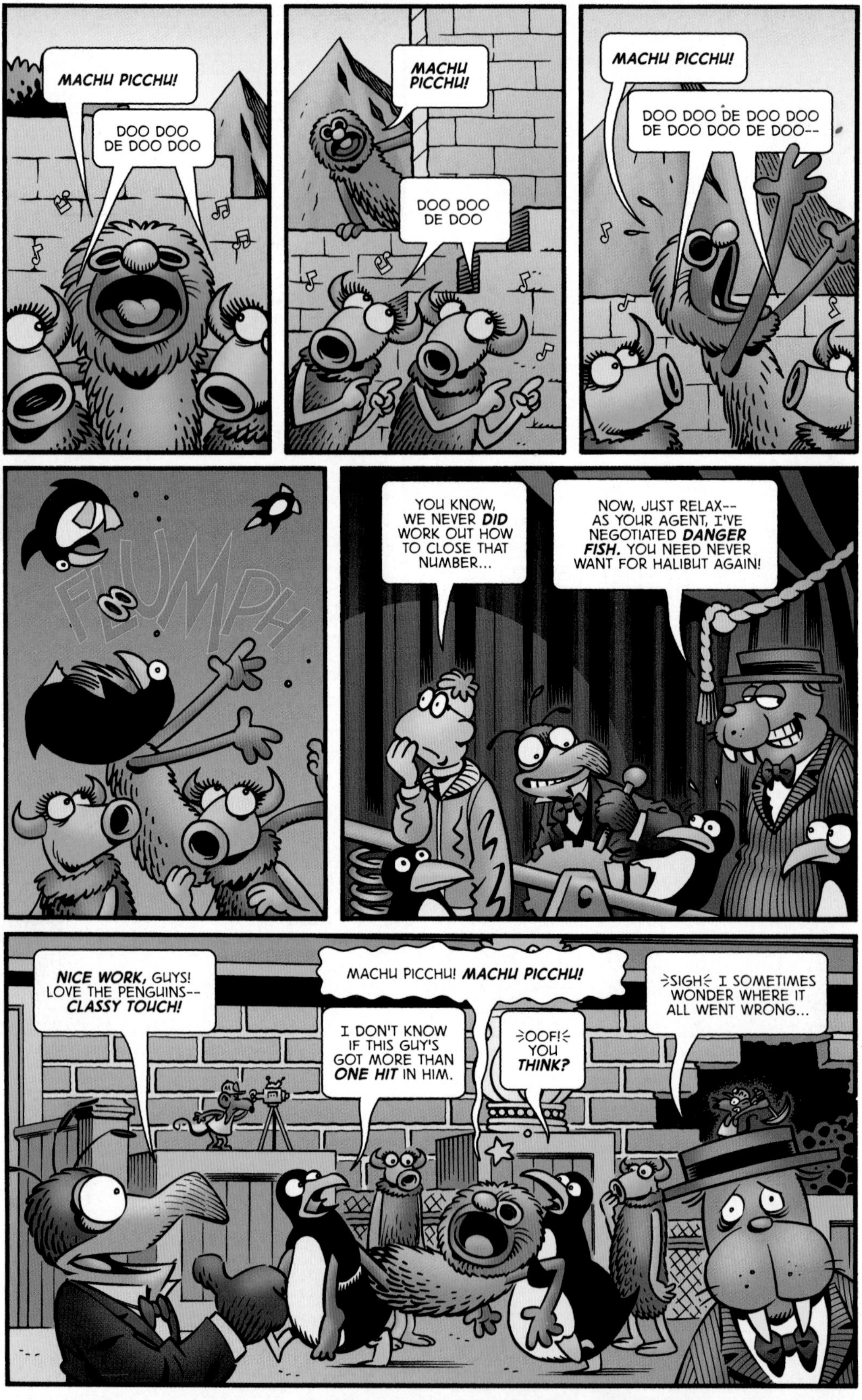
MACHU PICCHU!
DOO DOO DE DOO DOO
MACHU PICCHU!
DOO DOO DE DOO
MACHU PICCHU!
DOO DOO DE DOO DOO DE DOO DOO DE DOO--
FLUMPH
YOU KNOW, WE NEVER DID WORK OUT HOW TO CLOSE THAT NUMBER...
NOW, JUST RELAX-- AS YOUR AGENT, I'VE NEGOTIATED DANGER FISH. YOU NEED NEVER WANT FOR HALIBUT AGAIN!
NICE WORK, GUYS! LOVE THE PENGUINS-- CLASSY TOUCH!
MACHU PICCHU! MACHU PICCHU!
I DON'T KNOW IF THIS GUY'S GOT MORE THAN ONE HIT IN HIM.
OOF! YOU THINK?
SIGH I SOMETIMES WONDER WHERE IT ALL WENT WRONG...

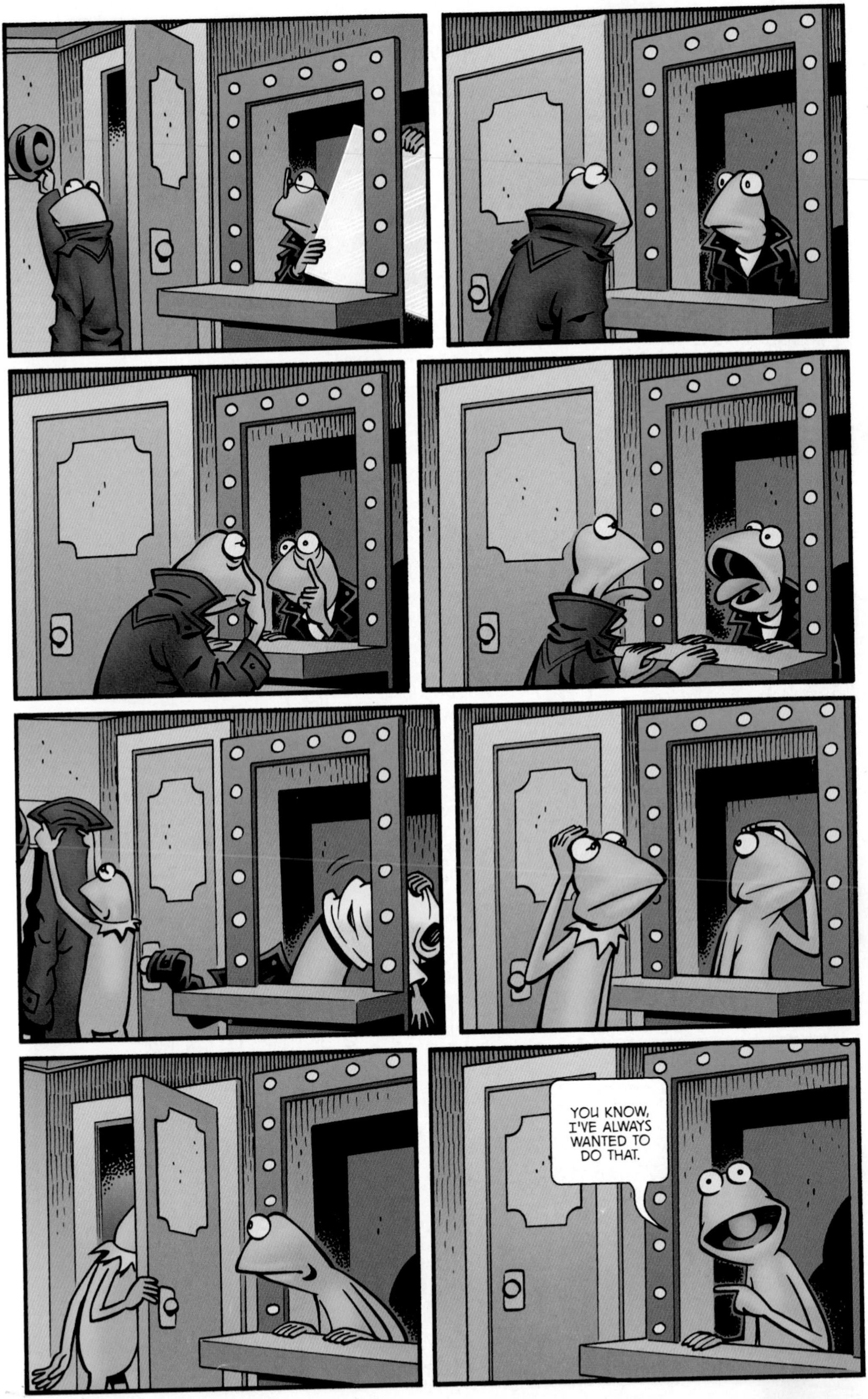
YOU KNOW, I'VE ALWAYS WANTED TO DO THAT.

GREETINGS—I'M LOOKING FOR THE *ELECTRIC MAYHEM* BAND...?

THAT'S US! I'M *DOCTOR TEETH.* AND YOU MUST BE T*HE HYPNOTIST?*

INDEED! *CREEPY MCBOO,* AT YOUR SERVICE! WHERE'S THE *PATIENT?*

THAT WOULD BE *ANIMAL,* OUR *DRUMMER* THERE.

YEAH. LI'L GUY LOST HIS *MOJO.* THINK YOU CAN *DO* SOMETHIN' ABOUT IT?

ONE CAN BUT *TRY!* NOW, ANIMAL—*WATCH THE WATCH!* YOU ARE GETTING SLEEPY...*SLEEEEPYYY...*

SLEEEPPYYY...

EXCELLENT! NOW— WHEN I SNAP MY FINGERS YOU WILL AWAKEN...AND YOUR DRUMMING WILL BE ON FIRE! *ON FIRE,* I SAY! ONE...TWO...THREE...

ZZZZZZZ

SNAP

HNNGH?

AAAGHH! *DRUMS! DRUMS!*

YOU'RE *COVERED,* BUDDY!

REMARKABLE! A PHYSICAL MANIFESTATION OF A *METAPHOR!* IT'S BEEN *YEARS* SINCE I HAD ONE OF THOSE...

SPEAKING OF *FIRED...!*

THIS ANY GOOD TO US, RIZZO?

HMM... NOT BAD. PUT IT WITH THE STASH.

FOR RAT

NEXT:

MUPPET LABS

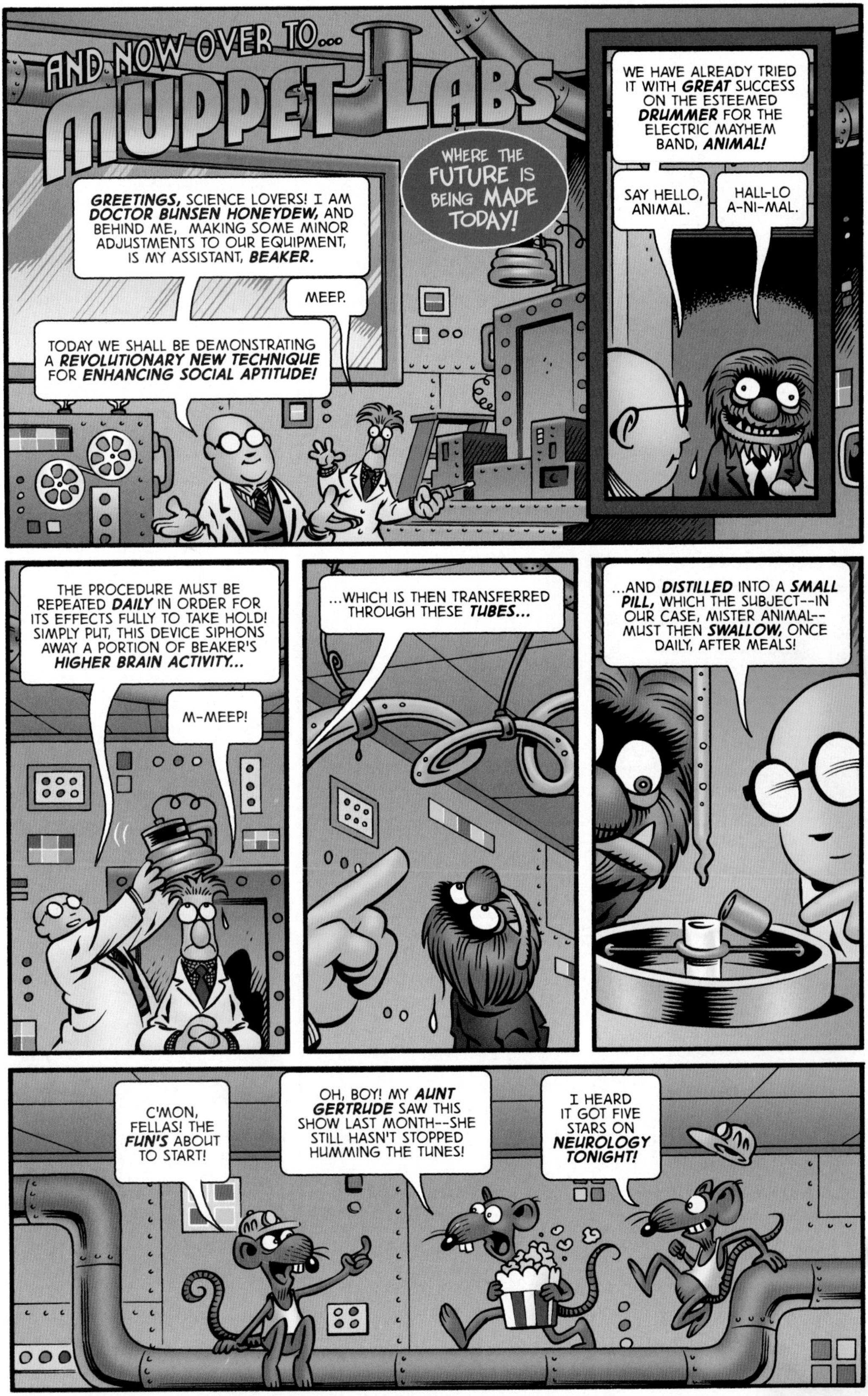
AND NOW OVER TO...
MUPPET LABS
WHERE THE FUTURE IS BEING MADE TODAY!
GREETINGS, SCIENCE LOVERS! I AM DOCTOR BUNSEN HONEYDEW, AND BEHIND ME, MAKING SOME MINOR ADJUSTMENTS TO OUR EQUIPMENT, IS MY ASSISTANT, BEAKER.
MEEP.
TODAY WE SHALL BE DEMONSTRATING A REVOLUTIONARY NEW TECHNIQUE FOR ENHANCING SOCIAL APTITUDE!
WE HAVE ALREADY TRIED IT WITH GREAT SUCCESS ON THE ESTEEMED DRUMMER FOR THE ELECTRIC MAYHEM BAND, ANIMAL!
SAY HELLO, ANIMAL.
HALL-LO A-NI-MAL.
THE PROCEDURE MUST BE REPEATED DAILY IN ORDER FOR ITS EFFECTS FULLY TO TAKE HOLD! SIMPLY PUT, THIS DEVICE SIPHONS AWAY A PORTION OF BEAKER'S HIGHER BRAIN ACTIVITY...
M-MEEP!
...WHICH IS THEN TRANSFERRED THROUGH THESE TUBES...
...AND DISTILLED INTO A SMALL PILL, WHICH THE SUBJECT--IN OUR CASE, MISTER ANIMAL--MUST THEN SWALLOW, ONCE DAILY, AFTER MEALS!
C'MON, FELLAS! THE FUN'S ABOUT TO START!
OH, BOY! MY AUNT GERTRUDE SAW THIS SHOW LAST MONTH--SHE STILL HASN'T STOPPED HUMMING THE TUNES!
I HEARD IT GOT FIVE STARS ON NEUROLOGY TONIGHT!

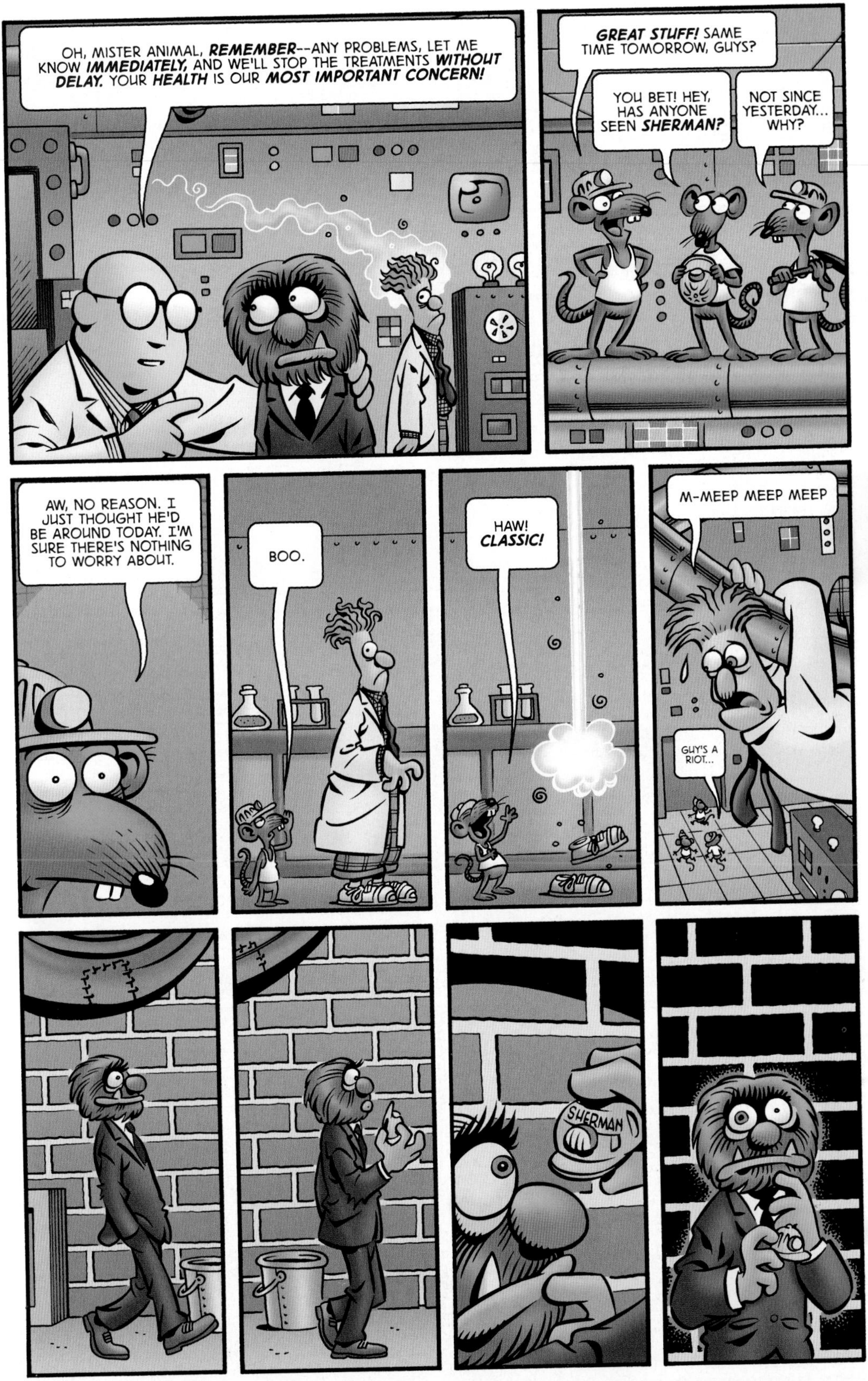

OH, MISTER ANIMAL, **REMEMBER**--ANY PROBLEMS, LET ME KNOW **IMMEDIATELY,** AND WE'LL STOP THE TREATMENTS **WITHOUT DELAY.** YOUR **HEALTH** IS OUR **MOST IMPORTANT CONCERN!**
GREAT STUFF! SAME TIME TOMORROW, GUYS?
YOU BET! HEY, HAS ANYONE SEEN **SHERMAN?**
NOT SINCE YESTERDAY... WHY?
AW, NO REASON. I JUST THOUGHT HE'D BE AROUND TODAY. I'M SURE THERE'S NOTHING TO WORRY ABOUT.
BOO.
HAW! **CLASSIC!**
M-MEEP MEEP MEEP
GUY'S A RIOT...
SHERMAN

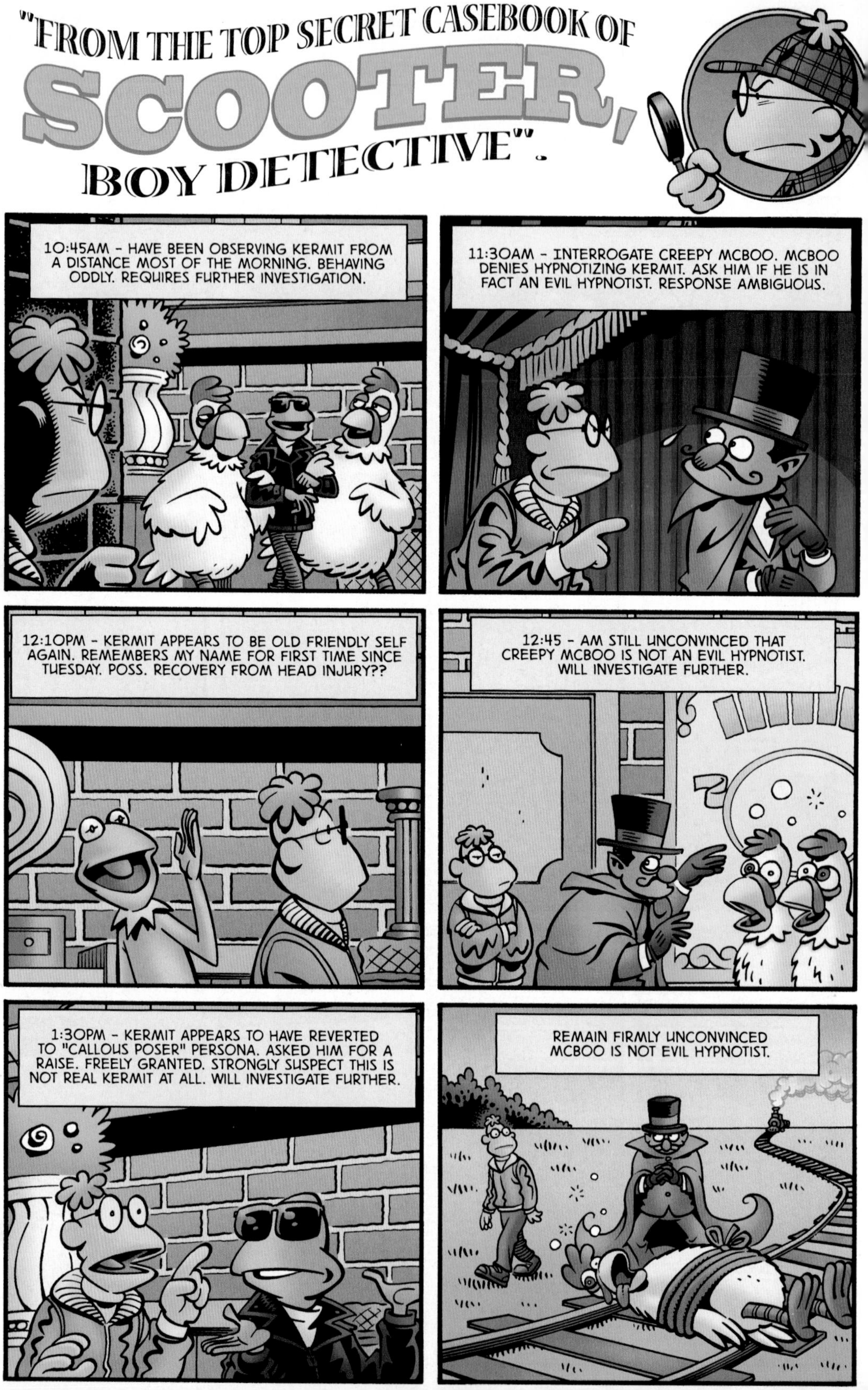
"FROM THE TOP SECRET CASEBOOK OF
SCOOTER,
BOY DETECTIVE".
10:45AM - HAVE BEEN OBSERVING KERMIT FROM A DISTANCE MOST OF THE MORNING. BEHAVING ODDLY. REQUIRES FURTHER INVESTIGATION.
11:30AM - INTERROGATE CREEPY MCBOO. MCBOO DENIES HYPNOTIZING KERMIT. ASK HIM IF HE IS IN FACT AN EVIL HYPNOTIST. RESPONSE AMBIGUOUS.
12:10PM - KERMIT APPEARS TO BE OLD FRIENDLY SELF AGAIN. REMEMBERS MY NAME FOR FIRST TIME SINCE TUESDAY. POSS. RECOVERY FROM HEAD INJURY??
12:45 - AM STILL UNCONVINCED THAT CREEPY MCBOO IS NOT AN EVIL HYPNOTIST. WILL INVESTIGATE FURTHER.
1:30PM - KERMIT APPEARS TO HAVE REVERTED TO "CALLOUS POSER" PERSONA. ASKED HIM FOR A RAISE. FREELY GRANTED. STRONGLY SUSPECT THIS IS NOT REAL KERMIT AT ALL. WILL INVESTIGATE FURTHER.
REMAIN FIRMLY UNCONVINCED MCBOO IS NOT EVIL HYPNOTIST.

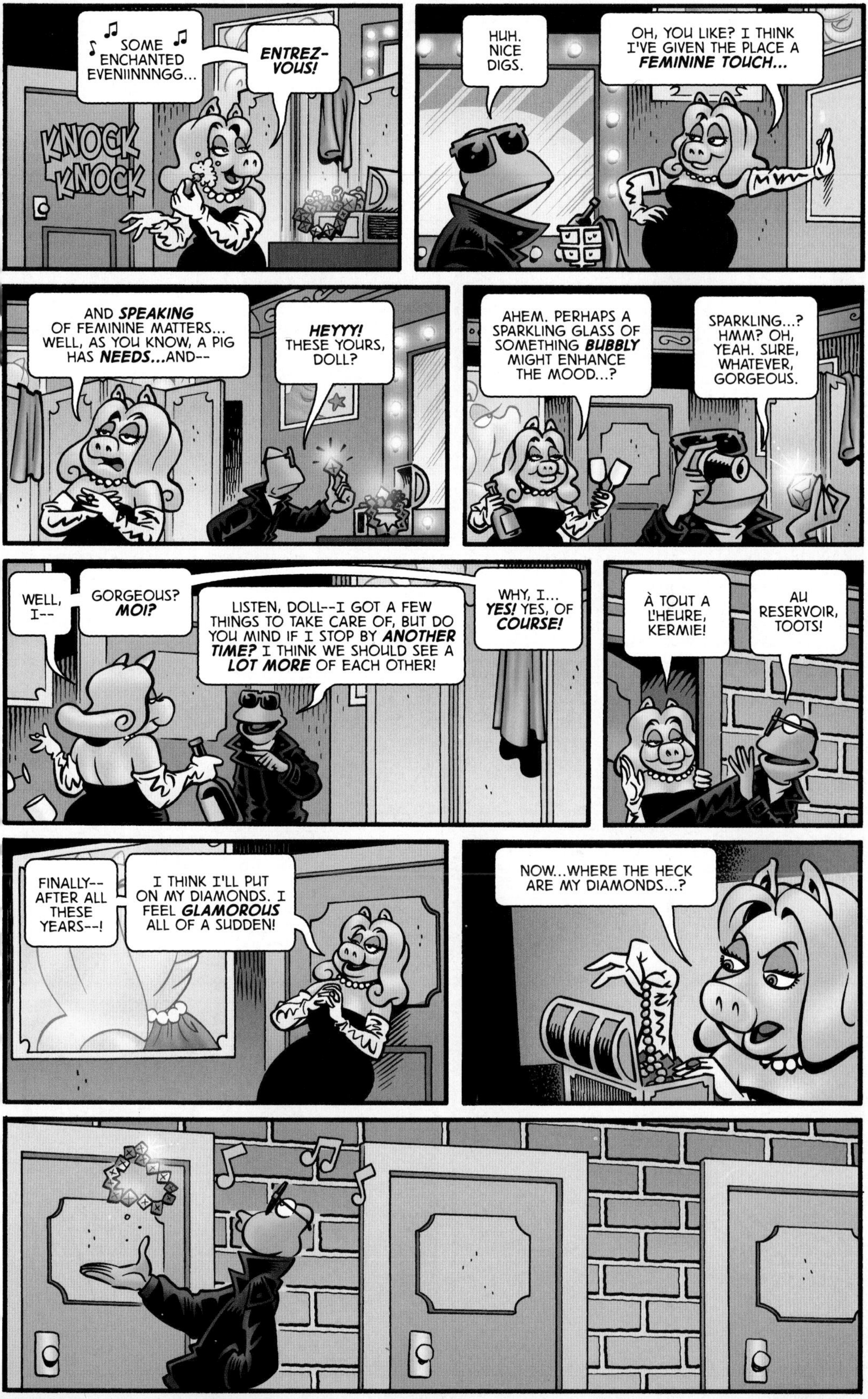
♪ ♫ SOME ♫ ENCHANTED EVENIINNNGG...
ENTREZ-VOUS!
KNOCK KNOCK
HUH. NICE DIGS.
OH, YOU LIKE? I THINK I'VE GIVEN THE PLACE A FEMININE TOUCH...
AND SPEAKING OF FEMININE MATTERS... WELL, AS YOU KNOW, A PIG HAS NEEDS...AND--
HEYYY! THESE YOURS, DOLL?
AHEM. PERHAPS A SPARKLING GLASS OF SOMETHING BUBBLY MIGHT ENHANCE THE MOOD...?
SPARKLING...? HMM? OH, YEAH. SURE, WHATEVER, GORGEOUS.
WELL, I--
GORGEOUS? MOI?
LISTEN, DOLL--I GOT A FEW THINGS TO TAKE CARE OF, BUT DO YOU MIND IF I STOP BY ANOTHER TIME? I THINK WE SHOULD SEE A LOT MORE OF EACH OTHER!
WHY, I... YES! YES, OF COURSE!
À TOUT A L'HEURE, KERMIE!
AU RESERVOIR, TOOTS!
FINALLY-- AFTER ALL THESE YEARS--!
I THINK I'LL PUT ON MY DIAMONDS. I FEEL GLAMOROUS ALL OF A SUDDEN!
NOW...WHERE THE HECK ARE MY DIAMONDS...?

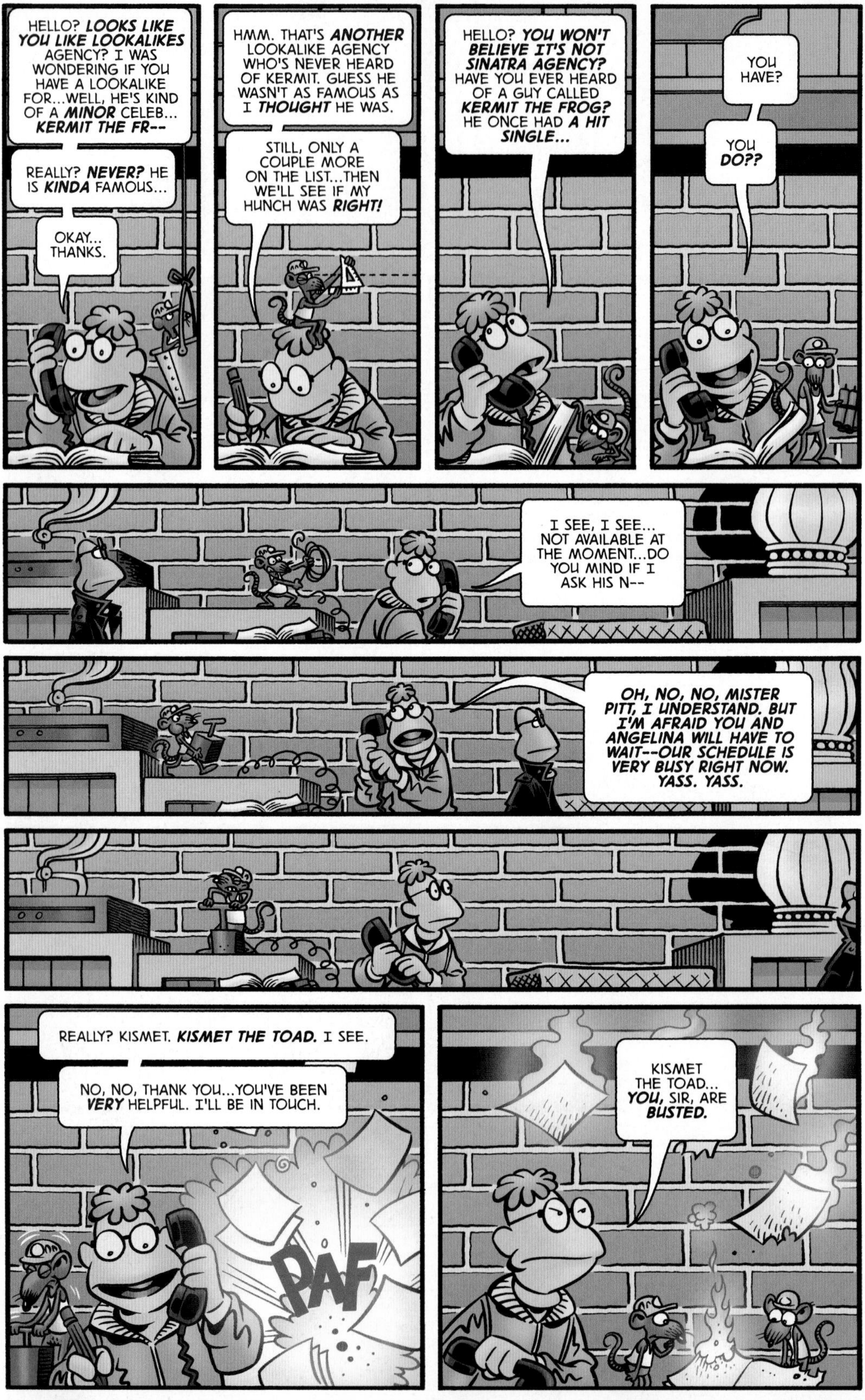
HELLO? LOOKS LIKE YOU LIKE LOOKALIKES AGENCY? I WAS WONDERING IF YOU HAVE A LOOKALIKE FOR...WELL, HE'S KIND OF A MINOR CELEB... KERMIT THE FR--
REALLY? NEVER? HE IS KINDA FAMOUS...
OKAY... THANKS.
HMM. THAT'S ANOTHER LOOKALIKE AGENCY WHO'S NEVER HEARD OF KERMIT. GUESS HE WASN'T AS FAMOUS AS I THOUGHT HE WAS.
STILL, ONLY A COUPLE MORE ON THE LIST...THEN WE'LL SEE IF MY HUNCH WAS RIGHT!
HELLO? YOU WON'T BELIEVE IT'S NOT SINATRA AGENCY? HAVE YOU EVER HEARD OF A GUY CALLED KERMIT THE FROG? HE ONCE HAD A HIT SINGLE...
YOU HAVE?
YOU DO??
I SEE, I SEE... NOT AVAILABLE AT THE MOMENT...DO YOU MIND IF I ASK HIS N--
OH, NO, NO, MISTER PITT, I UNDERSTAND. BUT I'M AFRAID YOU AND ANGELINA WILL HAVE TO WAIT--OUR SCHEDULE IS VERY BUSY RIGHT NOW. YASS. YASS.
REALLY? KISMET. KISMET THE TOAD. I SEE.
NO, NO, THANK YOU...YOU'VE BEEN VERY HELPFUL. I'LL BE IN TOUCH.
PAF
KISMET THE TOAD... YOU, SIR, ARE BUSTED.

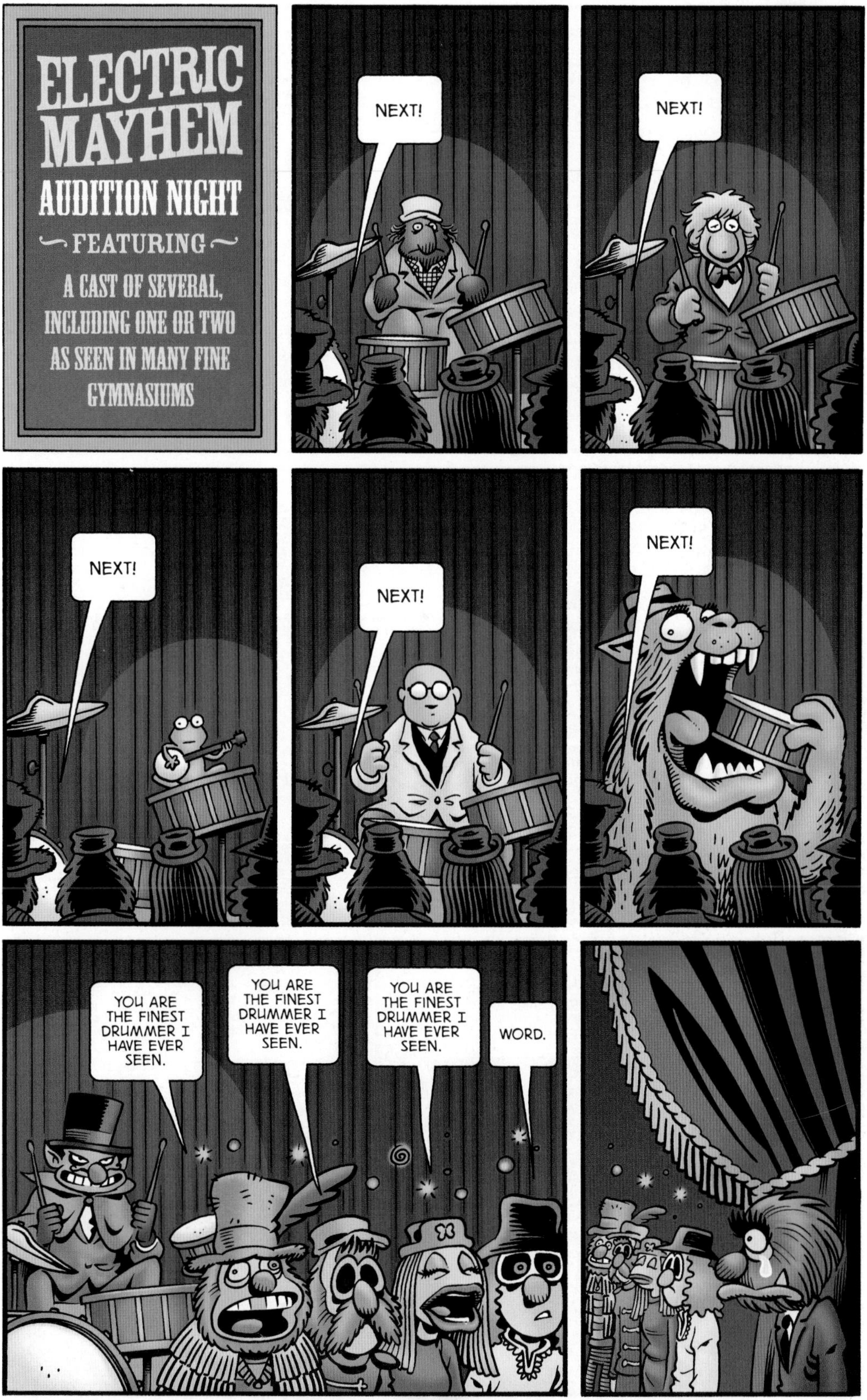
ELECTRIC MAYHEM
AUDITION NIGHT
FEATURING
A CAST OF SEVERAL, INCLUDING ONE OR TWO AS SEEN IN MANY FINE GYMNASIUMS
NEXT!
NEXT!
NEXT!
NEXT!
NEXT!
YOU ARE THE FINEST DRUMMER I HAVE EVER SEEN.
YOU ARE THE FINEST DRUMMER I HAVE EVER SEEN.
YOU ARE THE FINEST DRUMMER I HAVE EVER SEEN.
WORD.

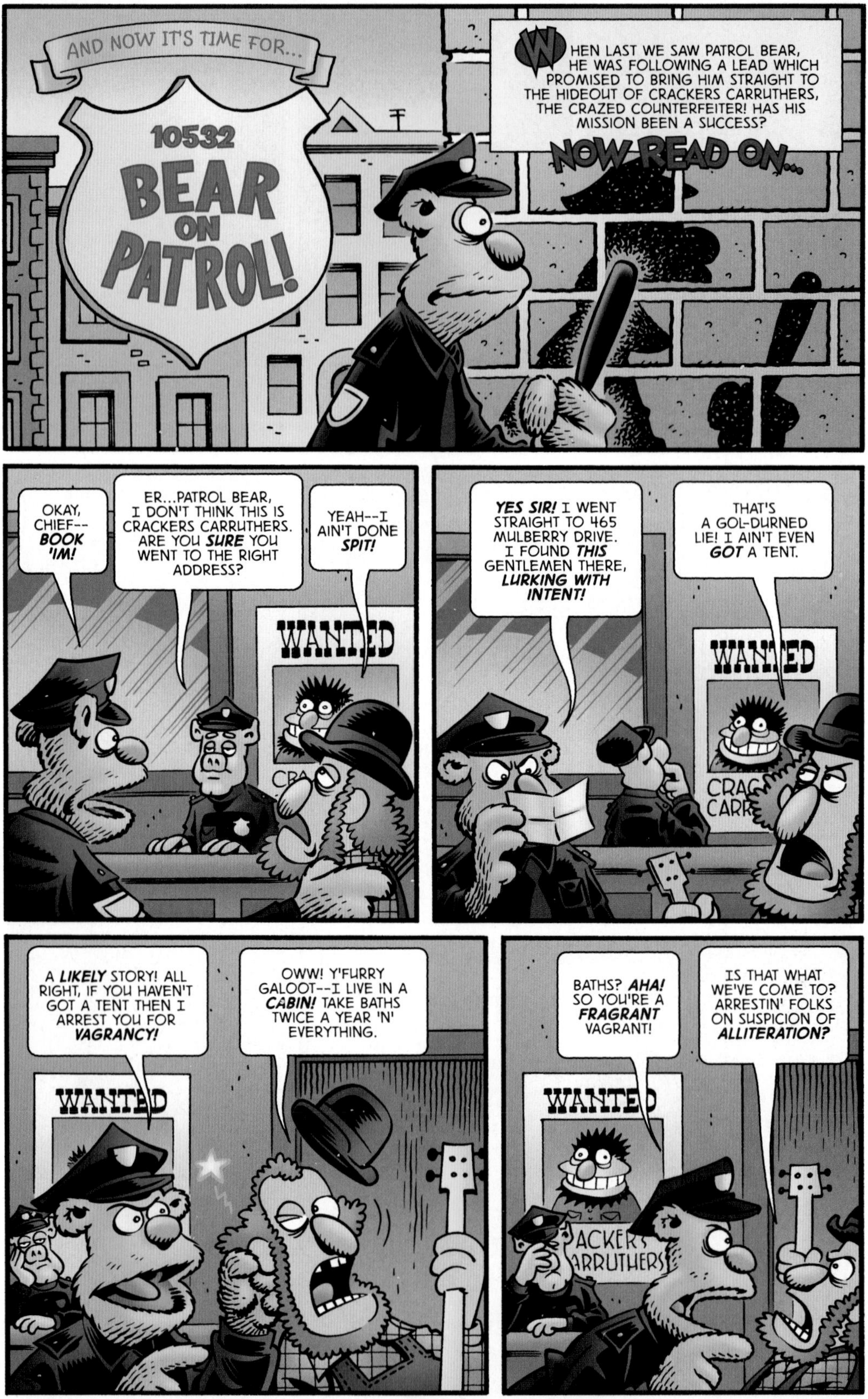
AND NOW IT'S TIME FOR...
10532
BEAR ON PATROL!
WHEN LAST WE SAW PATROL BEAR, HE WAS FOLLOWING A LEAD WHICH PROMISED TO BRING HIM STRAIGHT TO THE HIDEOUT OF CRACKERS CARRUTHERS, THE CRAZED COUNTERFEITER! HAS HIS MISSION BEEN A SUCCESS?
NOW READ ON...
OKAY, CHIEF-- BOOK 'IM!
ER...PATROL BEAR, I DON'T THINK THIS IS CRACKERS CARRUTHERS. ARE YOU SURE YOU WENT TO THE RIGHT ADDRESS?
YEAH--I AIN'T DONE SPIT!
WANTED
YES SIR! I WENT STRAIGHT TO 465 MULBERRY DRIVE. I FOUND THIS GENTLEMEN THERE, LURKING WITH INTENT!
THAT'S A GOL-DURNED LIE! I AIN'T EVEN GOT A TENT.
WANTED
A LIKELY STORY! ALL RIGHT, IF YOU HAVEN'T GOT A TENT THEN I ARREST YOU FOR VAGRANCY!
OWW! Y'FURRY GALOOT--I LIVE IN A CABIN! TAKE BATHS TWICE A YEAR 'N' EVERYTHING.
WANTED
BATHS? AHA! SO YOU'RE A FRAGRANT VAGRANT!
IS THAT WHAT WE'VE COME TO? ARRESTIN' FOLKS ON SUSPICION OF ALLITERATION?
WANTED

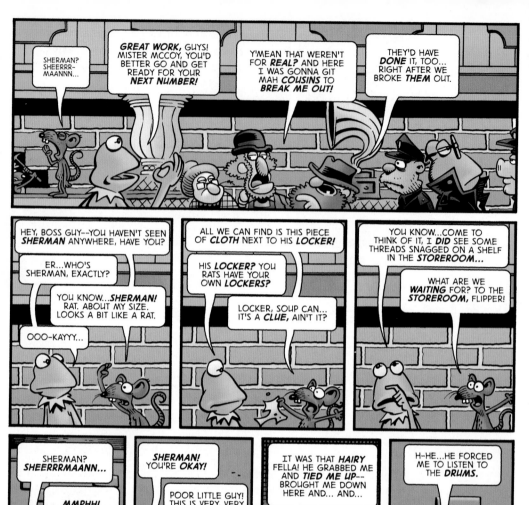

SHERMAN? SHEERRR- MAANNN...

GREAT WORK, GUYS! MISTER MCCOY, YOU'D BETTER GO AND GET READY FOR YOUR NEXT NUMBER!

Y'MEAN THAT WEREN'T FOR REAL? AND HERE I WAS GONNA GIT MAH COUSINS TO BREAK ME OUT!

THEY'D HAVE DONE IT, TOO... RIGHT AFTER WE BROKE THEM OUT.

HEY, BOSS GUY--YOU HAVEN'T SEEN SHERMAN ANYWHERE, HAVE YOU?

ER...WHO'S SHERMAN, EXACTLY?

YOU KNOW...SHERMAN! RAT. ABOUT MY SIZE. LOOKS A BIT LIKE A RAT.

OOO-KAYYY...

ALL WE CAN FIND IS THIS PIECE OF CLOTH NEXT TO HIS LOCKER!

HIS LOCKER? YOU RATS HAVE YOUR OWN LOCKERS?

LOCKER, SOUP CAN... IT'S A CLUE, AIN'T IT?

YOU KNOW...COME TO THINK OF IT, I DID SEE SOME THREADS SNAGGED ON A SHELF IN THE STOREROOM...

WHAT ARE WE WAITING FOR? TO THE STOREROOM, FLIPPER!

SHERMAN? SHEERRRMAANN...

MMPHH! MMMPPHH!

SHERMAN! YOU'RE OKAY!

POOR LITTLE GUY! THIS IS VERY, VERY STRANGE...

IT WAS THAT HAIRY FELLA! HE GRABBED ME AND TIED ME UP-- BROUGHT ME DOWN HERE AND... AND...

WHAT? WHAT??

H-HE...HE FORCED ME TO LISTEN TO THE DRUMS.

SHERMAN

ANIMAL

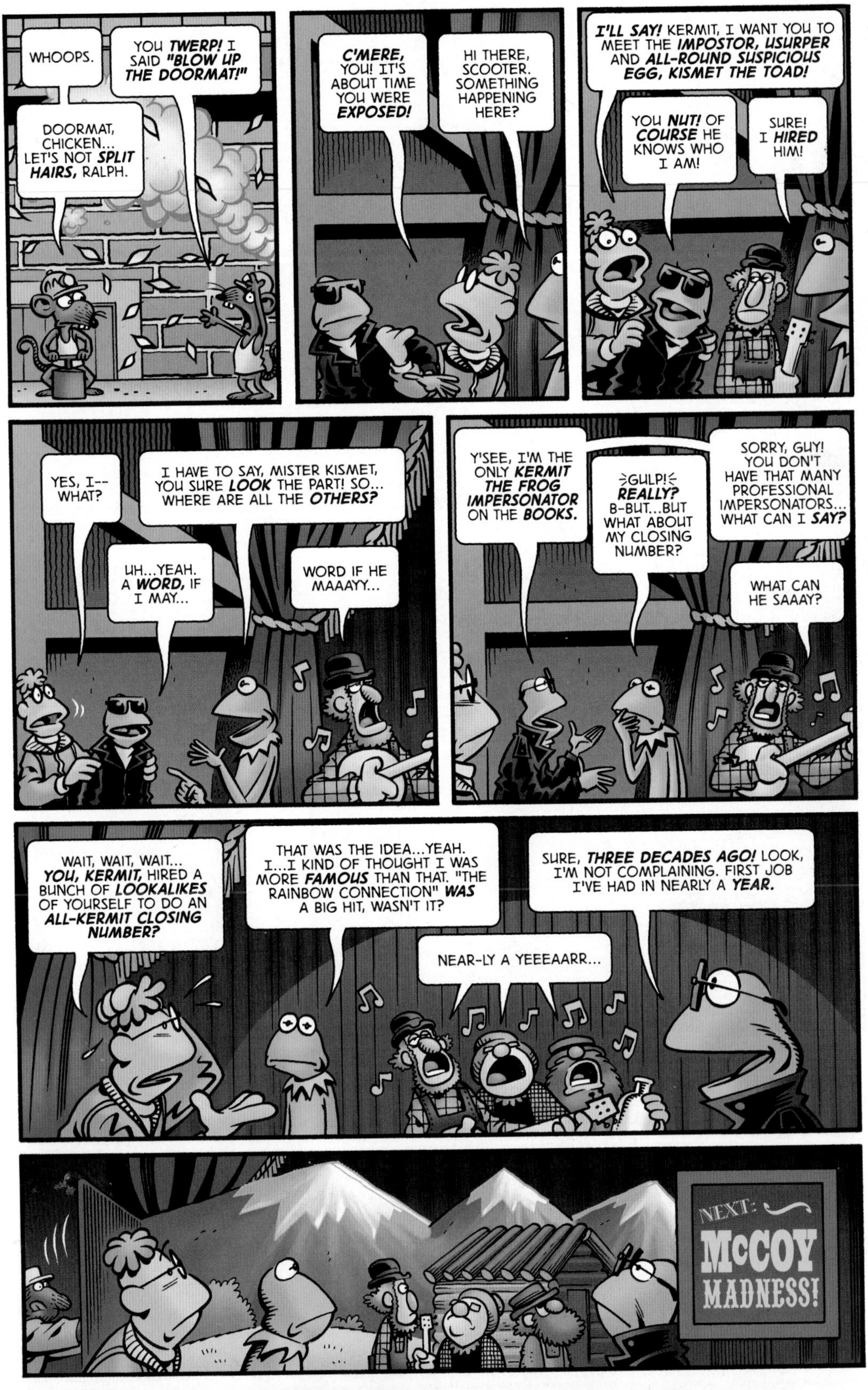
WHOOPS.
YOU TWERP! I SAID "BLOW UP THE DOORMAT!"
DOORMAT, CHICKEN... LET'S NOT SPLIT HAIRS, RALPH.
C'MERE, YOU! IT'S ABOUT TIME YOU WERE EXPOSED!
HI THERE, SCOOTER. SOMETHING HAPPENING HERE?
I'LL SAY! KERMIT, I WANT YOU TO MEET THE IMPOSTOR, USURPER AND ALL-ROUND SUSPICIOUS EGG, KISMET THE TOAD!
YOU NUT! OF COURSE HE KNOWS WHO I AM!
SURE! I HIRED HIM!
YES, I-- WHAT?
I HAVE TO SAY, MISTER KISMET, YOU SURE LOOK THE PART! SO... WHERE ARE ALL THE OTHERS?
UH...YEAH. A WORD, IF I MAY...
WORD IF HE MAAAYY...
Y'SEE, I'M THE ONLY KERMIT THE FROG IMPERSONATOR ON THE BOOKS.
GULP! REALLY? B-BUT...BUT WHAT ABOUT MY CLOSING NUMBER?
SORRY, GUY! YOU DON'T HAVE THAT MANY PROFESSIONAL IMPERSONATORS... WHAT CAN I SAY?
WHAT CAN HE SAAAY?
WAIT, WAIT, WAIT... YOU, KERMIT, HIRED A BUNCH OF LOOKALIKES OF YOURSELF TO DO AN ALL-KERMIT CLOSING NUMBER?
THAT WAS THE IDEA...YEAH. I...I KIND OF THOUGHT I WAS MORE FAMOUS THAN THAT. "THE RAINBOW CONNECTION" WAS A BIG HIT, WASN'T IT?
SURE, THREE DECADES AGO! LOOK, I'M NOT COMPLAINING. FIRST JOB I'VE HAD IN NEARLY A YEAR.
NEAR-LY A YEEEAARR...
NEXT: McCOY MADNESS!

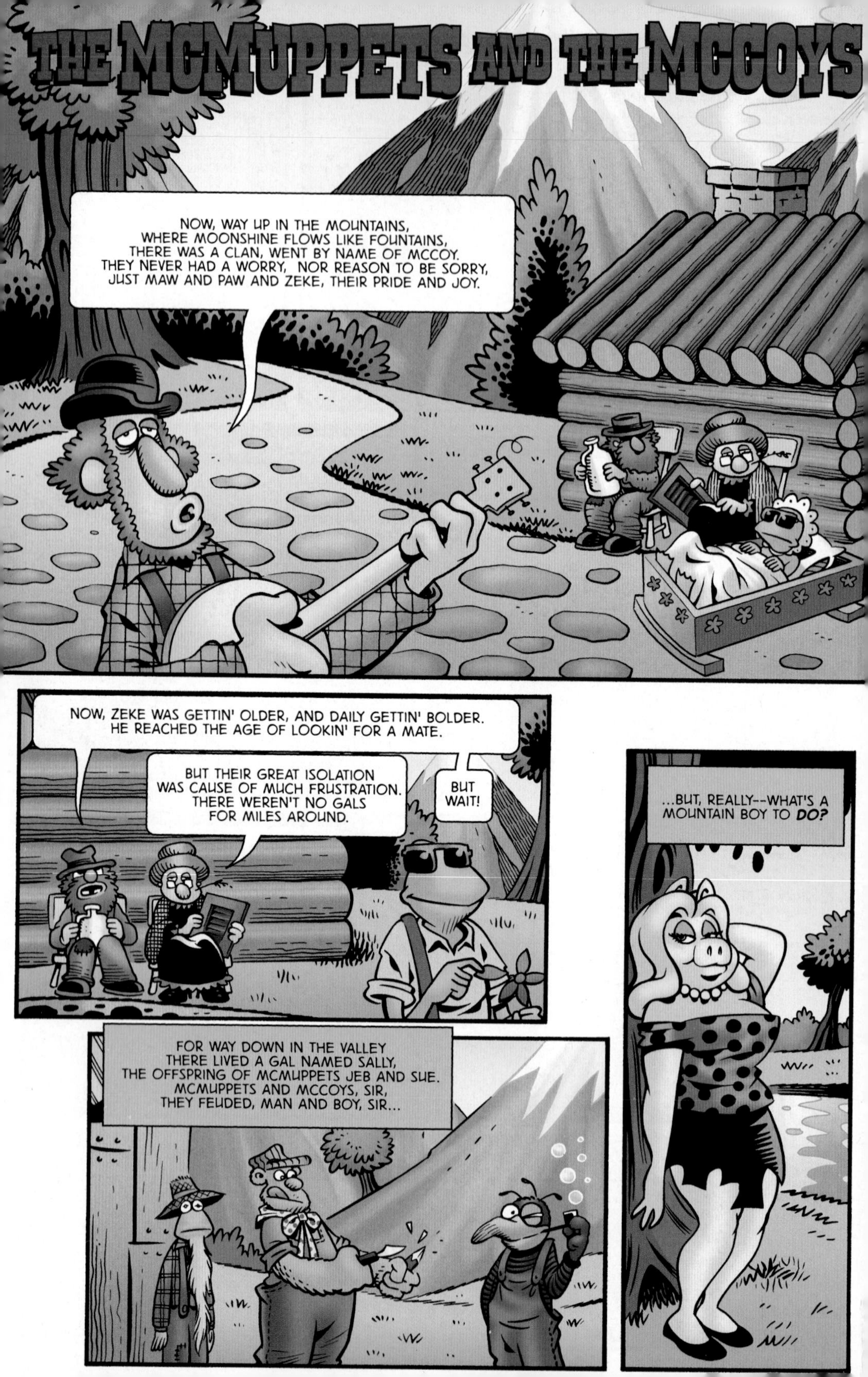
THE MCMUPPETS AND THE MCCOYS
NOW, WAY UP IN THE MOUNTAINS, WHERE MOONSHINE FLOWS LIKE FOUNTAINS, THERE WAS A CLAN, WENT BY NAME OF MCCOY. THEY NEVER HAD A WORRY, NOR REASON TO BE SORRY, JUST MAW AND PAW AND ZEKE, THEIR PRIDE AND JOY.
NOW, ZEKE WAS GETTIN' OLDER, AND DAILY GETTIN' BOLDER. HE REACHED THE AGE OF LOOKIN' FOR A MATE.
BUT THEIR GREAT ISOLATION WAS CAUSE OF MUCH FRUSTRATION. THERE WEREN'T NO GALS FOR MILES AROUND.
BUT WAIT!
...BUT, REALLY--WHAT'S A MOUNTAIN BOY TO *DO?*
FOR WAY DOWN IN THE VALLEY THERE LIVED A GAL NAMED SALLY, THE OFFSPRING OF MCMUPPETS JEB AND SUE. MCMUPPETS AND MCCOYS, SIR, THEY FEUDED, MAN AND BOY, SIR...

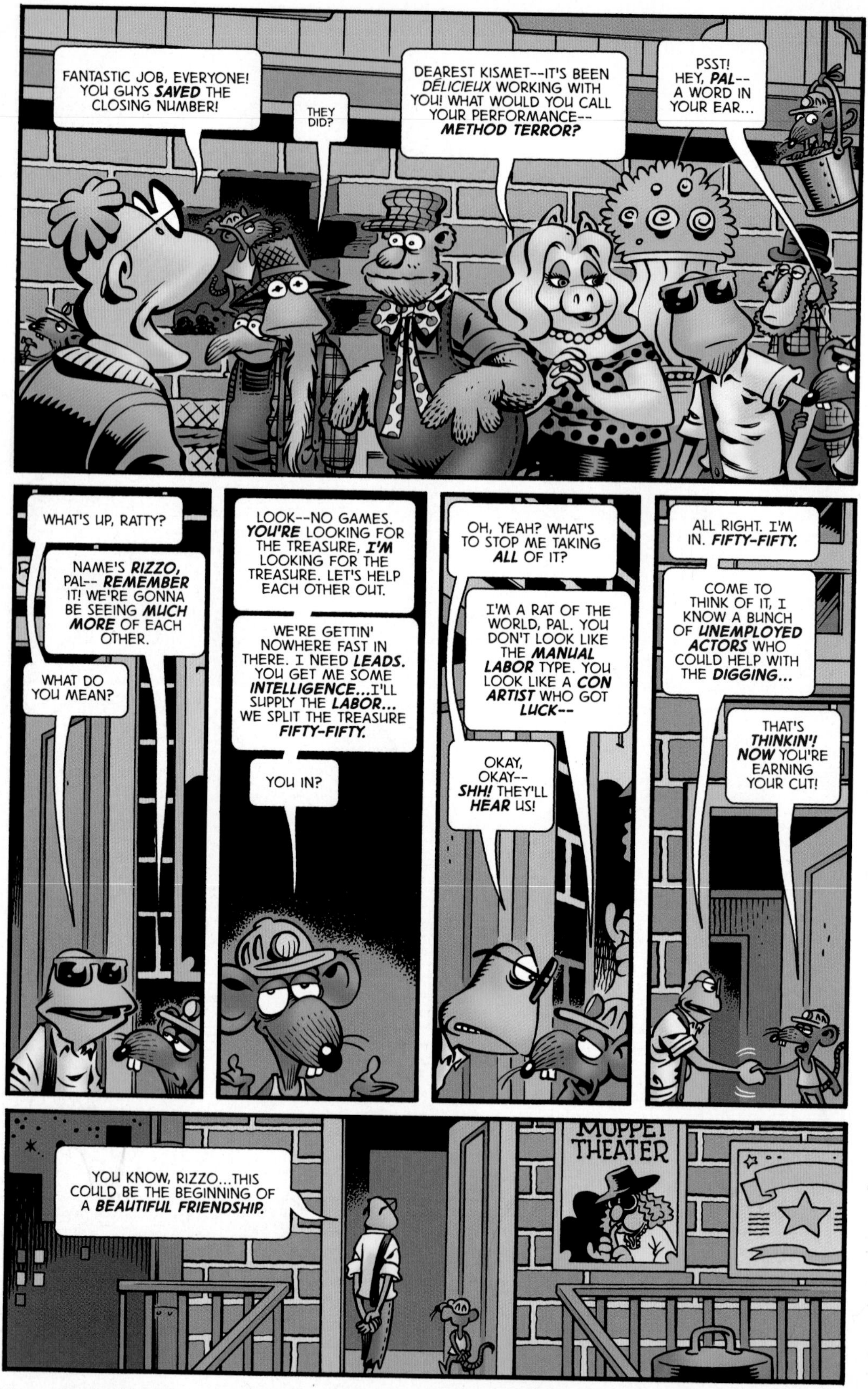
FANTASTIC JOB, EVERYONE! YOU GUYS SAVED THE CLOSING NUMBER!
THEY DID?
DEAREST KISMET--IT'S BEEN DÉLICIEUX WORKING WITH YOU! WHAT WOULD YOU CALL YOUR PERFORMANCE-- METHOD TERROR?
PSST! HEY, PAL-- A WORD IN YOUR EAR...
WHAT'S UP, RATTY?
NAME'S RIZZO, PAL-- REMEMBER IT! WE'RE GONNA BE SEEING MUCH MORE OF EACH OTHER.
WHAT DO YOU MEAN?
LOOK--NO GAMES. YOU'RE LOOKING FOR THE TREASURE, I'M LOOKING FOR THE TREASURE. LET'S HELP EACH OTHER OUT.
WE'RE GETTIN' NOWHERE FAST IN THERE. I NEED LEADS. YOU GET ME SOME INTELLIGENCE...I'LL SUPPLY THE LABOR... WE SPLIT THE TREASURE FIFTY-FIFTY.
YOU IN?
OH, YEAH? WHAT'S TO STOP ME TAKING ALL OF IT?
I'M A RAT OF THE WORLD, PAL. YOU DON'T LOOK LIKE THE MANUAL LABOR TYPE. YOU LOOK LIKE A CON ARTIST WHO GOT LUCK--
OKAY, OKAY-- SHH! THEY'LL HEAR US!
ALL RIGHT. I'M IN. FIFTY-FIFTY.
COME TO THINK OF IT, I KNOW A BUNCH OF UNEMPLOYED ACTORS WHO COULD HELP WITH THE DIGGING...
THAT'S THINKIN'! NOW YOU'RE EARNING YOUR CUT!
YOU KNOW, RIZZO...THIS COULD BE THE BEGINNING OF A BEAUTIFUL FRIENDSHIP.
MUPPET THEATER

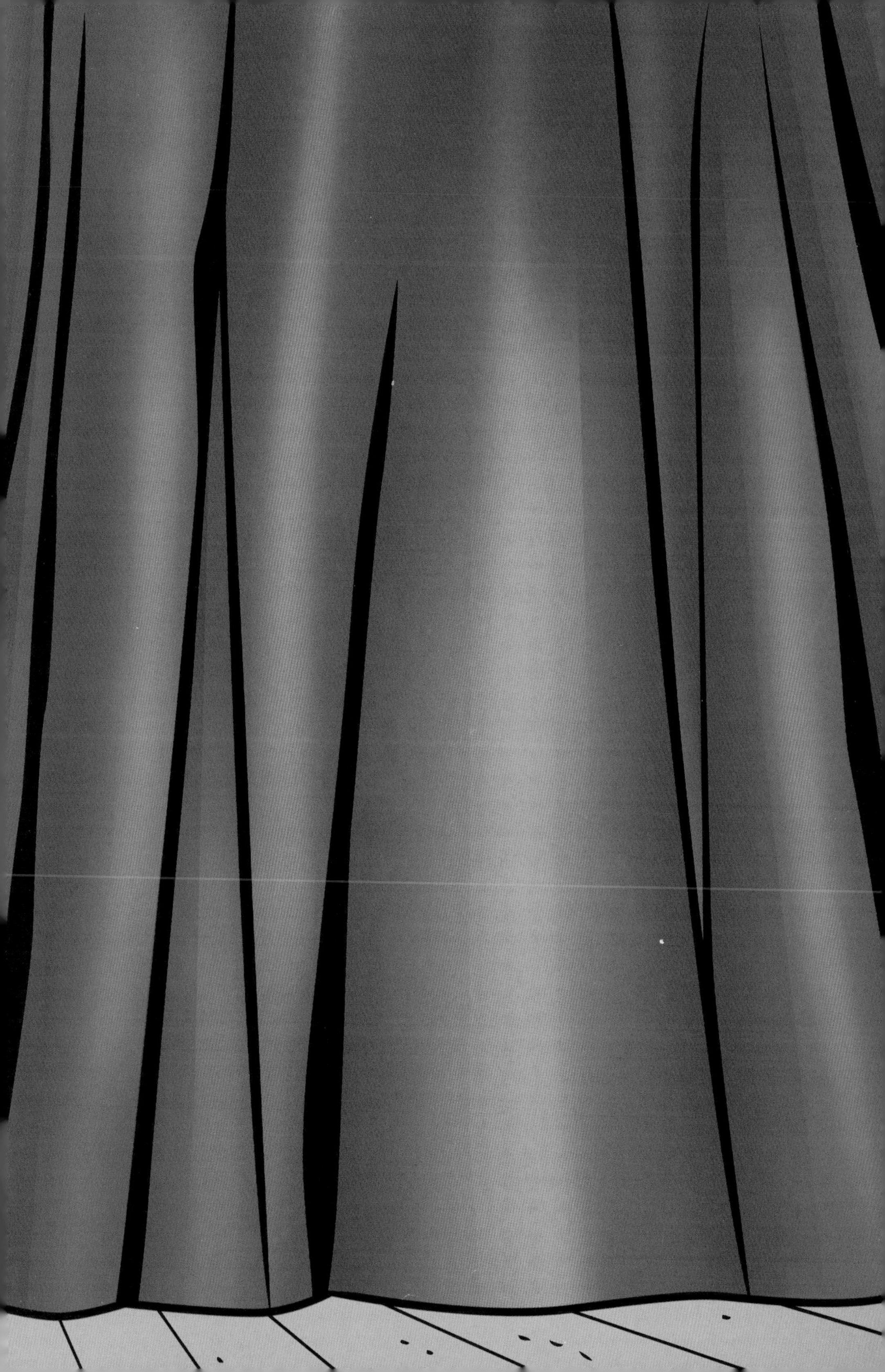

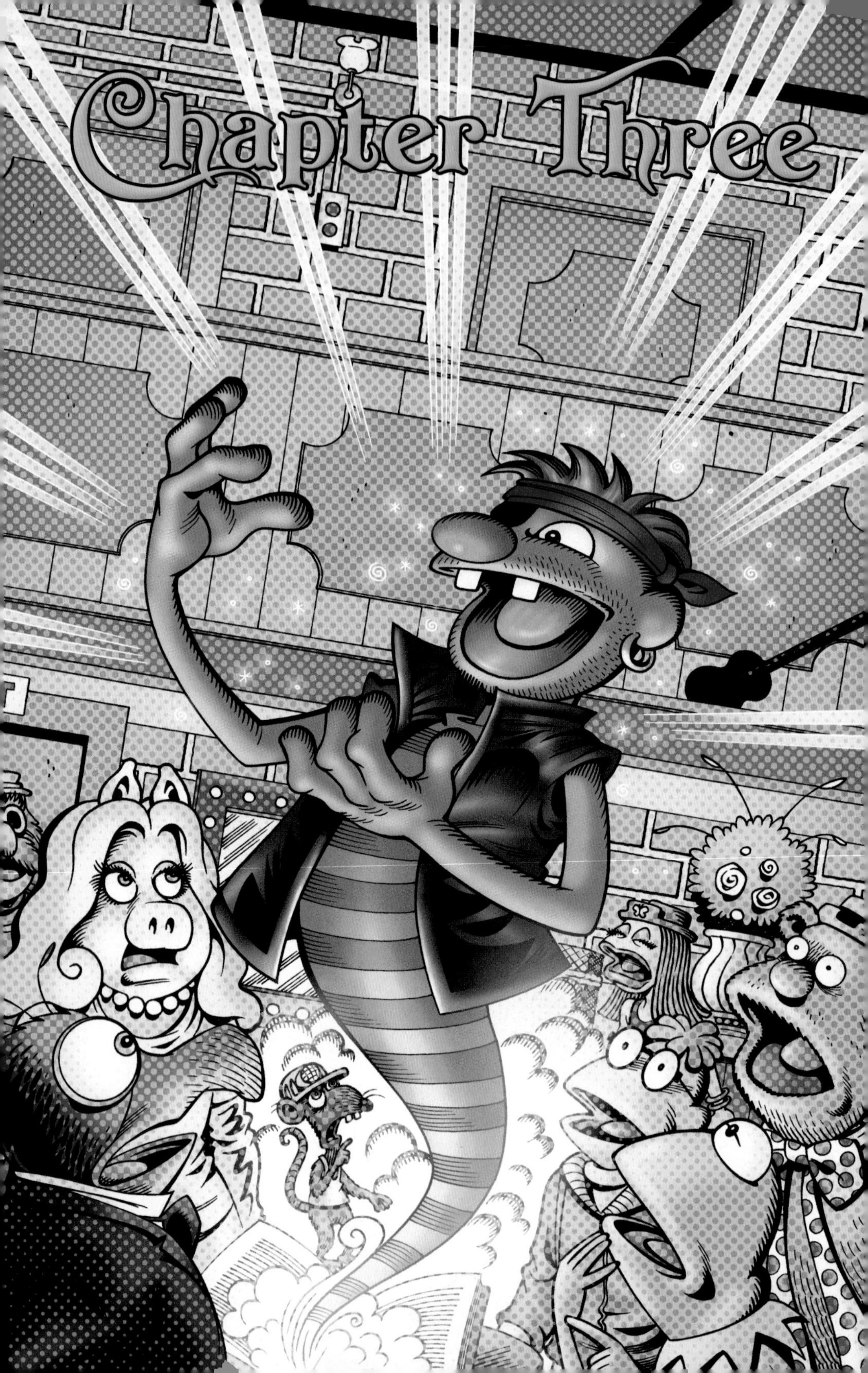
Chapter Three

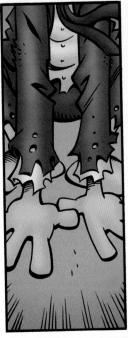

AND I'LL HAVE THAT SHOE **BACK** WHEN YOU REGAIN CONSCIOUSNESS, THANK YOU **VERY** MUCH! I'VE HEARD BETTER DRUM SOLOS **FALLING DOWN STAIRS!**

SHE'S NOT KIDDING!

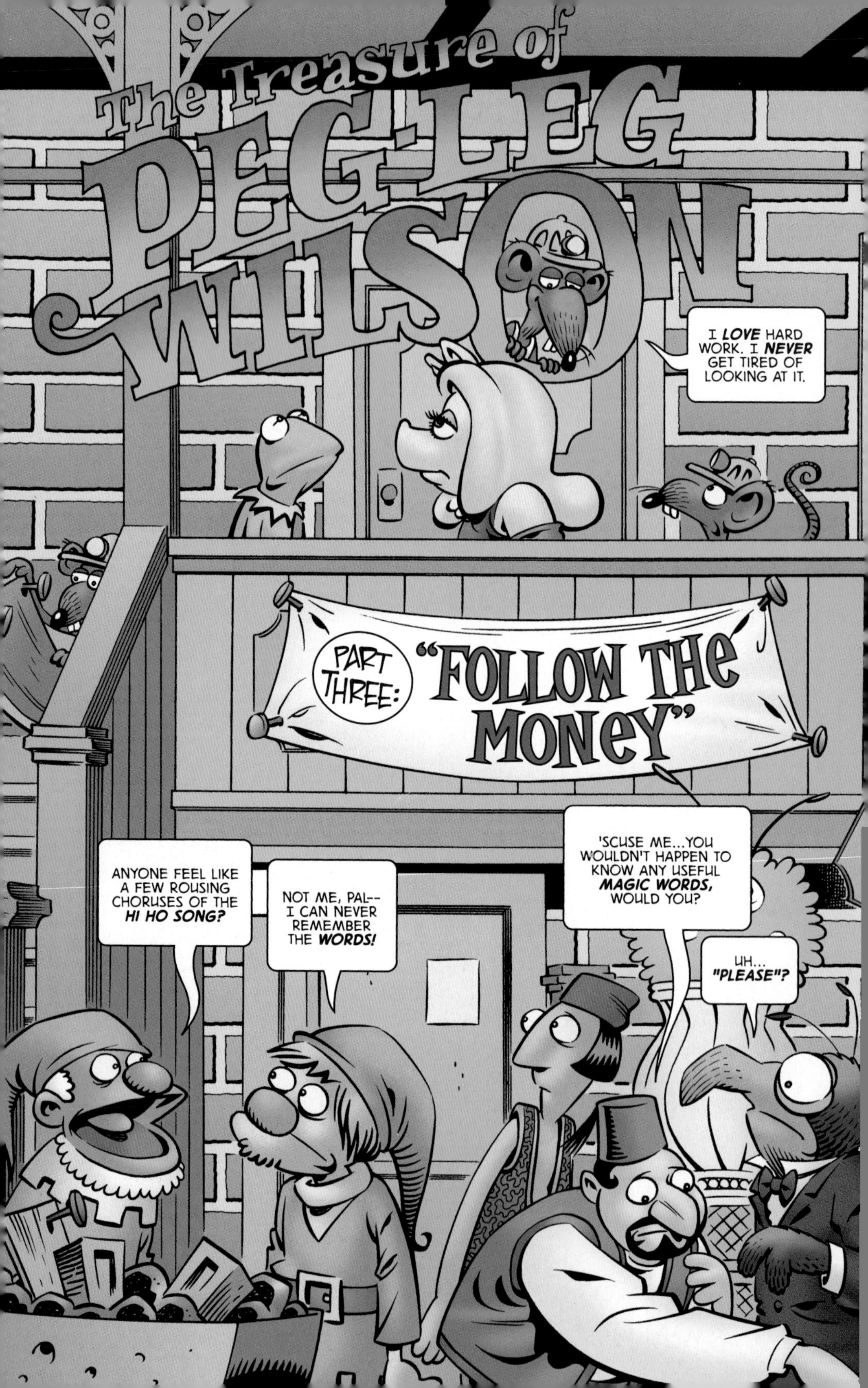
The Treasure of PEG-LEG WILSON
I LOVE HARD WORK. I NEVER GET TIRED OF LOOKING AT IT.
PART THREE: "FOLLOW THE MONEY"
ANYONE FEEL LIKE A FEW ROUSING CHORUSES OF THE HI HO SONG?
NOT ME, PAL-- I CAN NEVER REMEMBER THE WORDS!
'SCUSE ME...YOU WOULDN'T HAPPEN TO KNOW ANY USEFUL MAGIC WORDS, WOULD YOU?
UH... "PLEASE"?

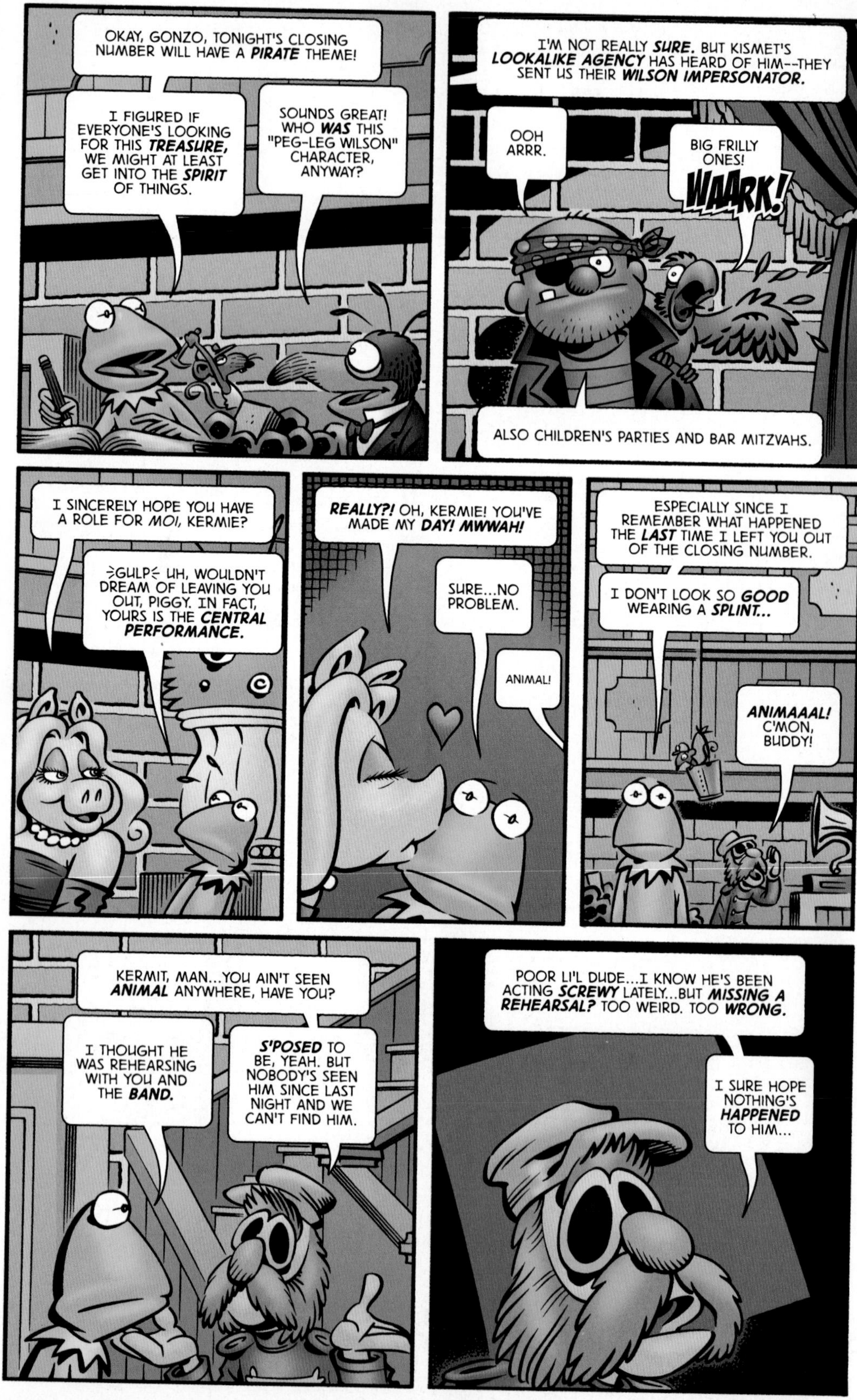

OKAY, GONZO, TONIGHT'S CLOSING NUMBER WILL HAVE A *PIRATE* THEME!
I FIGURED IF EVERYONE'S LOOKING FOR THIS *TREASURE,* WE MIGHT AT LEAST GET INTO THE *SPIRIT* OF THINGS.
SOUNDS GREAT! WHO *WAS* THIS "PEG-LEG WILSON" CHARACTER, ANYWAY?
I'M NOT REALLY *SURE.* BUT KISMET'S *LOOKALIKE AGENCY* HAS HEARD OF HIM--THEY SENT US THEIR *WILSON IMPERSONATOR.*
OOH ARRR.
BIG FRILLY ONES!
WAARK!
ALSO CHILDREN'S PARTIES AND BAR MITZVAHS.
I SINCERELY HOPE YOU HAVE A ROLE FOR *MOI,* KERMIE?
GULP UH, WOULDN'T DREAM OF LEAVING YOU OUT, PIGGY. IN FACT, YOURS IS THE *CENTRAL PERFORMANCE.*
REALLY?! OH, KERMIE! YOU'VE MADE MY *DAY! MWWAH!*
SURE...NO PROBLEM.
ANIMAL!
ESPECIALLY SINCE I REMEMBER WHAT HAPPENED THE *LAST* TIME I LEFT YOU OUT OF THE CLOSING NUMBER.
I DON'T LOOK SO *GOOD* WEARING A *SPLINT...*
ANIMAAAL! C'MON, BUDDY!
KERMIT, MAN...YOU AIN'T SEEN *ANIMAL* ANYWHERE, HAVE YOU?
I THOUGHT HE WAS REHEARSING WITH YOU AND THE *BAND.*
S'POSED TO BE, YEAH. BUT NOBODY'S SEEN HIM SINCE LAST NIGHT AND WE CAN'T FIND HIM.
POOR LI'L DUDE...I KNOW HE'S BEEN ACTING *SCREWY* LATELY...BUT *MISSING A REHEARSAL?* TOO WEIRD. TOO *WRONG.*
I SURE HOPE NOTHING'S *HAPPENED* TO HIM...

ANIMALOPOLY!

START

Doctor Honeydew gives you a pill which civilizes you.

ROLL AGAIN!

Your drumming deteriorates.

LOSE A TURN.

Band replaces you for an evening.

LOSE A TURN.

Experience strange blackout and wake up with rat-sized helmet in pocket.

SHERMAN

TAKE YOUR MEDICINE.

BACK TWO SQUARES!

Join golf club and give Dr Teeth bummer major.

£3

Read Tolstoy.

ROLL AGAIN!

WAR and PEACE

Acquire interest in Buddhism.

HAVE ANOTHER LIFE.

Wake up in storeroom clutching broken drumstick with clothes in rags.

TAKE YOUR MEDICINE.

Beaker's higher brain functions are distilled into pill form twice in one day.

LOSE A TURN

Forget to take pill and have another blackout.

LOSE A DAY.

Doctor Honeydew gives you today's dose of civilization.

TAKE YOUR MEDICINE.

Floyd discovers you hiding in a closet.

LOSE A TURN.

"BUDDY! BEEN LOOKING ALL OVER FOR YOU!"

END

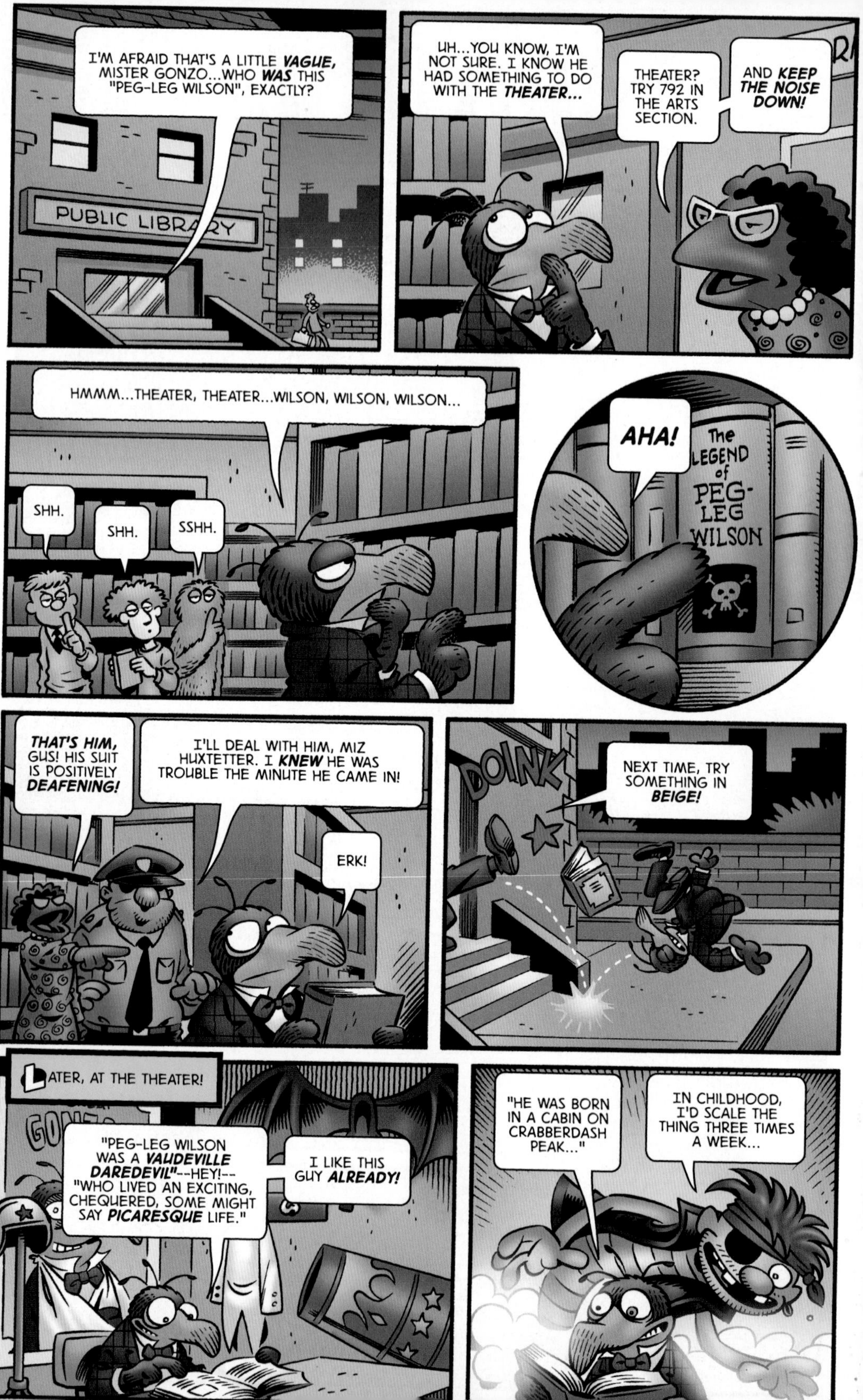

I'M AFRAID THAT'S A LITTLE VAGUE, MISTER GONZO...WHO WAS THIS "PEG-LEG WILSON", EXACTLY?
PUBLIC LIBRARY
UH...YOU KNOW, I'M NOT SURE. I KNOW HE HAD SOMETHING TO DO WITH THE THEATER...
THEATER? TRY 792 IN THE ARTS SECTION.
AND KEEP THE NOISE DOWN!
HMMM...THEATER, THEATER...WILSON, WILSON, WILSON...
SHH.
SHH.
SSHH.
AHA!
The LEGEND of PEG-LEG WILSON
THAT'S HIM, GUS! HIS SUIT IS POSITIVELY DEAFENING!
I'LL DEAL WITH HIM, MIZ HUXTETTER. I KNEW HE WAS TROUBLE THE MINUTE HE CAME IN!
ERK!
DOINK
NEXT TIME, TRY SOMETHING IN BEIGE!
LATER, AT THE THEATER!
"PEG-LEG WILSON WAS A VAUDEVILLE DAREDEVIL"--HEY!--"WHO LIVED AN EXCITING, CHEQUERED, SOME MIGHT SAY PICARESQUE LIFE."
I LIKE THIS GUY ALREADY!
"HE WAS BORN IN A CABIN ON CRABBERDASH PEAK..."
IN CHILDHOOD, I'D SCALE THE THING THREE TIMES A WEEK...

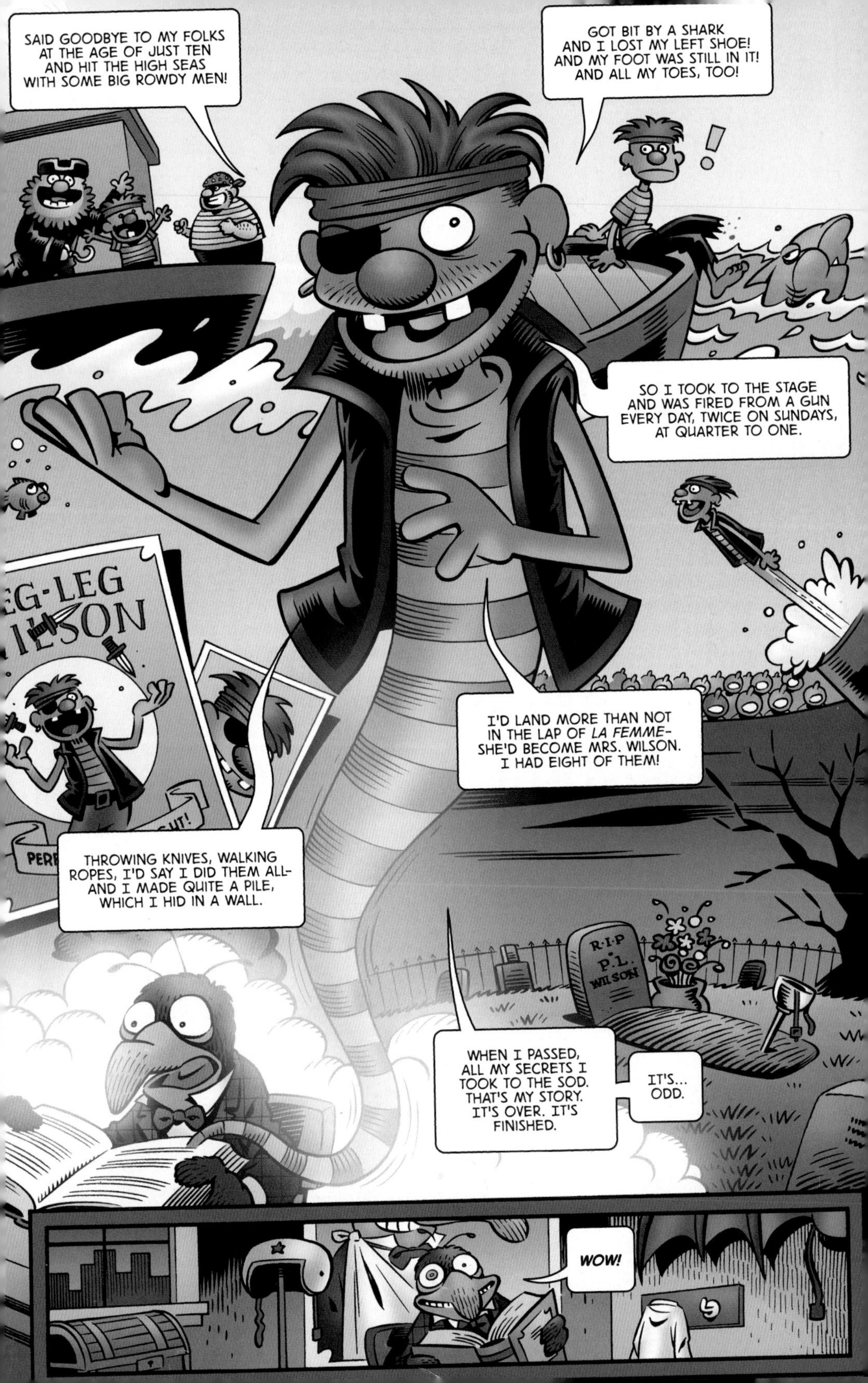
SAID GOODBYE TO MY FOLKS AT THE AGE OF JUST TEN AND HIT THE HIGH SEAS WITH SOME BIG ROWDY MEN!
GOT BIT BY A SHARK AND I LOST MY LEFT SHOE! AND MY FOOT WAS STILL IN IT! AND ALL MY TOES, TOO!
!
SO I TOOK TO THE STAGE AND WAS FIRED FROM A GUN EVERY DAY, TWICE ON SUNDAYS, AT QUARTER TO ONE.
EG-LEG
ILSON
PERF
GHT!
THROWING KNIVES, WALKING ROPES, I'D SAY I DID THEM ALL- AND I MADE QUITE A PILE, WHICH I HID IN A WALL.
I'D LAND MORE THAN NOT IN THE LAP OF *LA FEMME*- SHE'D BECOME MRS. WILSON. I HAD EIGHT OF THEM!
R·I·P
P.L.
WILSON
WHEN I PASSED, ALL MY SECRETS I TOOK TO THE SOD. THAT'S MY STORY. IT'S OVER. IT'S FINISHED.
IT'S... ODD.
WOW!

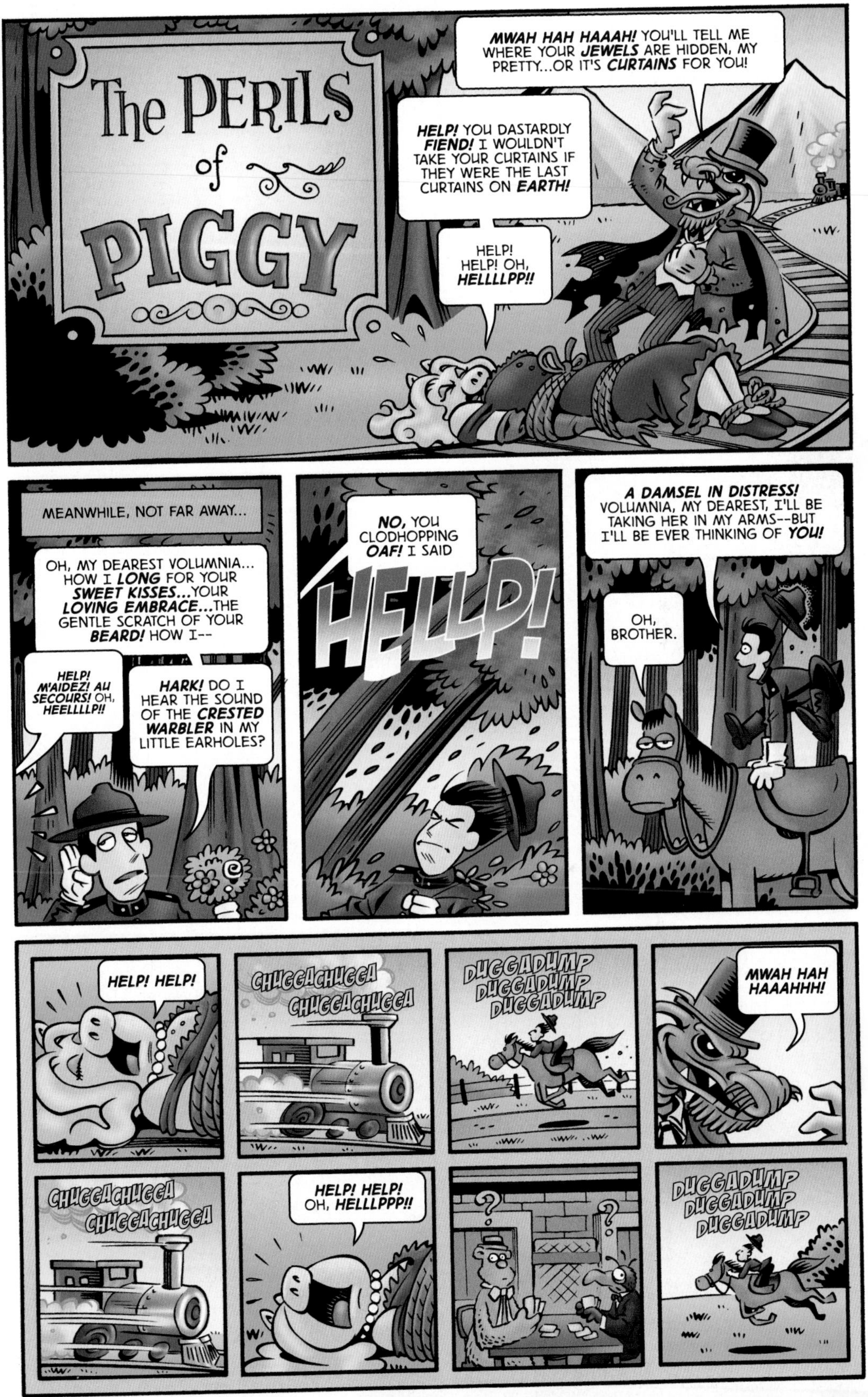

The PERILS of PIGGY
MWAH HAH HAAAH! YOU'LL TELL ME WHERE YOUR JEWELS ARE HIDDEN, MY PRETTY...OR IT'S CURTAINS FOR YOU!
HELP! YOU DASTARDLY FIEND! I WOULDN'T TAKE YOUR CURTAINS IF THEY WERE THE LAST CURTAINS ON EARTH!
HELP! HELP! OH, HELLLLPP!!
MEANWHILE, NOT FAR AWAY...
OH, MY DEAREST VOLUMNIA... HOW I LONG FOR YOUR SWEET KISSES...YOUR LOVING EMBRACE...THE GENTLE SCRATCH OF YOUR BEARD! HOW I--
HELP! M'AIDEZ! AU SECOURS! OH, HEELLLLP!!
HARK! DO I HEAR THE SOUND OF THE CRESTED WARBLER IN MY LITTLE EARHOLES?
NO, YOU CLODHOPPING OAF! I SAID
HELLP!
A DAMSEL IN DISTRESS! VOLUMNIA, MY DEAREST, I'LL BE TAKING HER IN MY ARMS--BUT I'LL BE EVER THINKING OF YOU!
OH, BROTHER.
HELP! HELP!
CHUGGACHUGGA CHUGGACHUGGA
DUGGADUMP DUGGADUMP DUGGADUMP
MWAH HAH HAAAHHH!
CHUGGACHUGGA CHUGGACHUGGA
HELP! HELP! OH, HELLLPPP!!
?
?
DUGGADUMP DUGGADUMP DUGGADUMP

WELL, I'LL BE HORNSWAGGLED!

SCREEEECH

OH! *MY HERO!*

EHH, THANKS ALL THE SAME, HORSE GUY, BUT I'VE GOT THIS COVERED...

CHUGGA CHUGGA CHUGGA CHUGGA CHUGGA CHUGGA CHUGG

YOU *WONDERFUL* MAN! HOW CAN I EVER *REPAY* YOU?

OH, I DON'T KNOW...I THINK IT WOULD BE REWARD ENOUGH TO SEE YOU WEARING THOSE *JEWELS* HE WAS AFTER.

OR PERHAPS... A LITTLE *KISS*...?

OR PERHAPS SEEING YOU WEARING THOSE *JEWELS* HE WAS AFTER.

B-BUT... BUT...

MOVE ON, ROMEO. JUST WALK AWAY.

GOTTA GO!

OH, YOU DARLING! WHY... OF *COURSE* I'LL WEAR THOSE JEWELS FOR YOU! UNTIL THEN...*ADIEU!*

AND NOW, I *TOO* MUST FLY. ON, ROCINANTE!

?

ERK!

DUGGADUMP
DUGGADUMP
DUGGADUMP
DUGGADUMP

ER...READ ANY GOOD BOOKS LATELY?

NAH.

WILL KISMET EVER GET TO SEE THOSE JEWELS?

WILL MISS PIGGY RETURN WAYNE'S HORSE IN GOOD EATING CONDITION?

WHAT *HAS UNCLE DEADLY BEEN READING LATELY?* BE HERE NEXT TIME, WHEN YOU'LL FIND OUT THE ANSWERS TO A BUNCH OF *COMPLETELY DIFFERENT* QUESTIONS ON...

The PERILS of
PIGGY

NOW WASH YOUR HANDS.

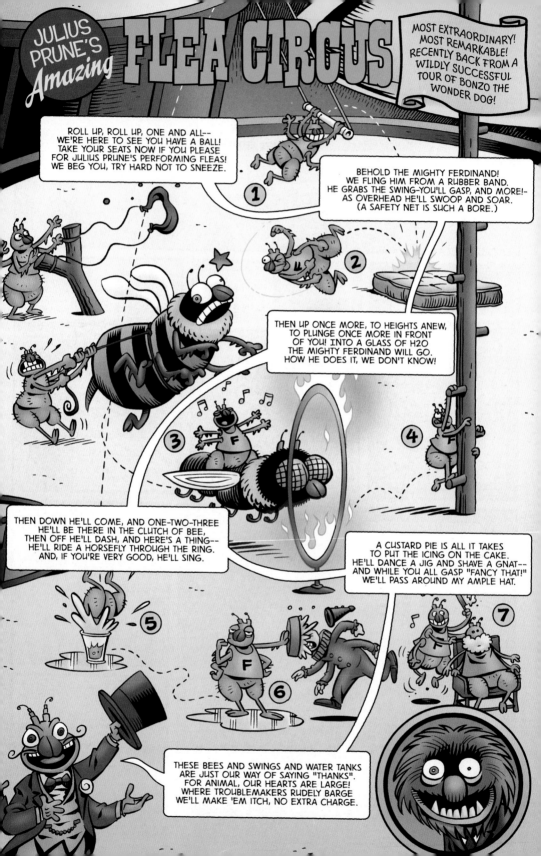

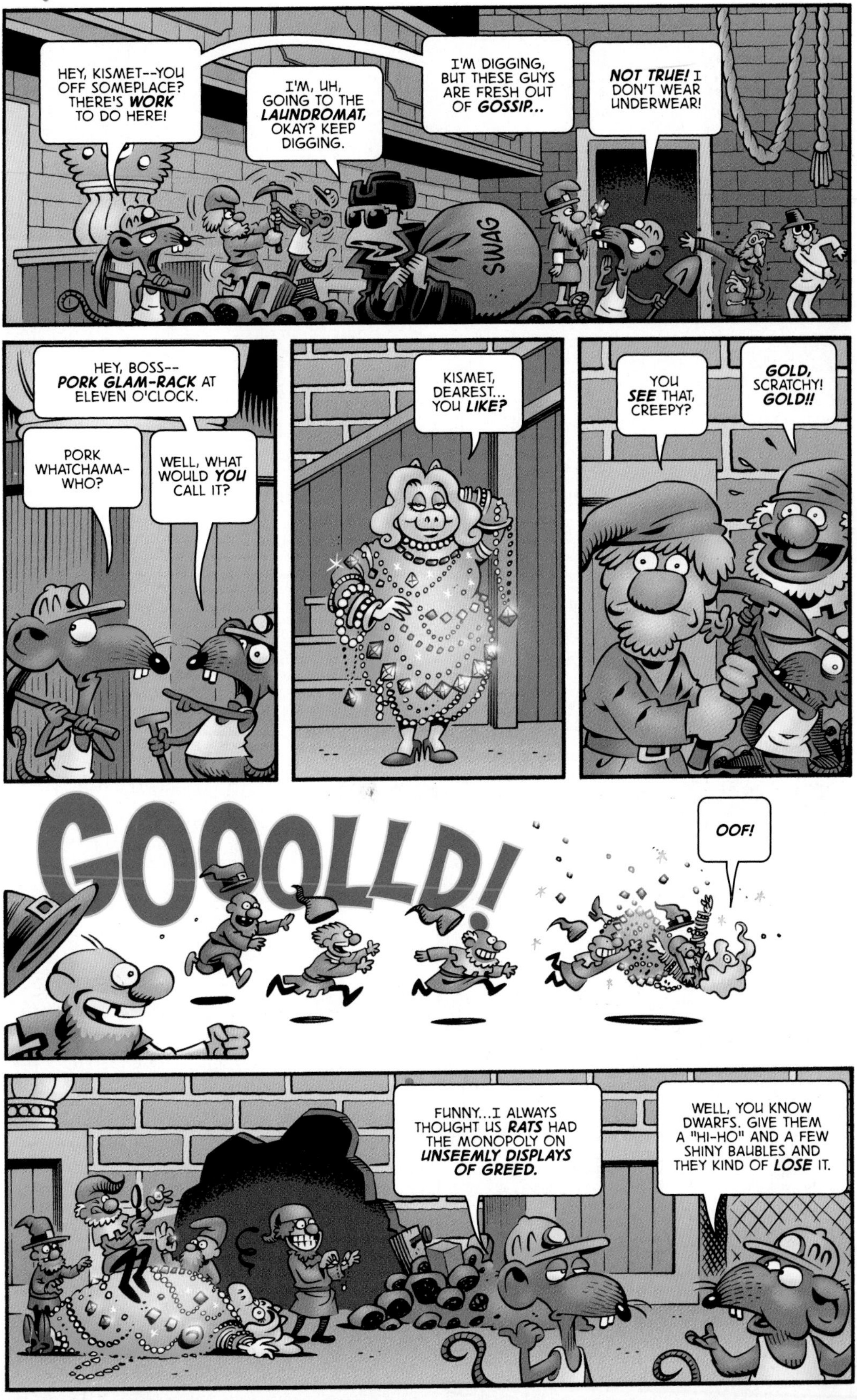
HEY, KISMET--YOU OFF SOMEPLACE? THERE'S **WORK** TO DO HERE!
I'M, UH, GOING TO THE **LAUNDROMAT,** OKAY? KEEP DIGGING.
I'M DIGGING, BUT THESE GUYS ARE FRESH OUT OF **GOSSIP...**
NOT TRUE! I DON'T WEAR UNDERWEAR!
SWAG
HEY, BOSS-- **PORK GLAM-RACK** AT ELEVEN O'CLOCK.
PORK WHATCHAMA-WHO?
WELL, WHAT WOULD **YOU** CALL IT?
KISMET, DEAREST... YOU **LIKE?**
YOU **SEE** THAT, CREEPY?
GOLD, SCRATCHY! **GOLD!!**
GOOOLLD!
OOF!
FUNNY...I ALWAYS THOUGHT US **RATS** HAD THE MONOPOLY ON **UNSEEMLY DISPLAYS OF GREED.**
WELL, YOU KNOW DWARFS. GIVE THEM A "HI-HO" AND A FEW SHINY BAUBLES AND THEY KIND OF **LOSE** IT.

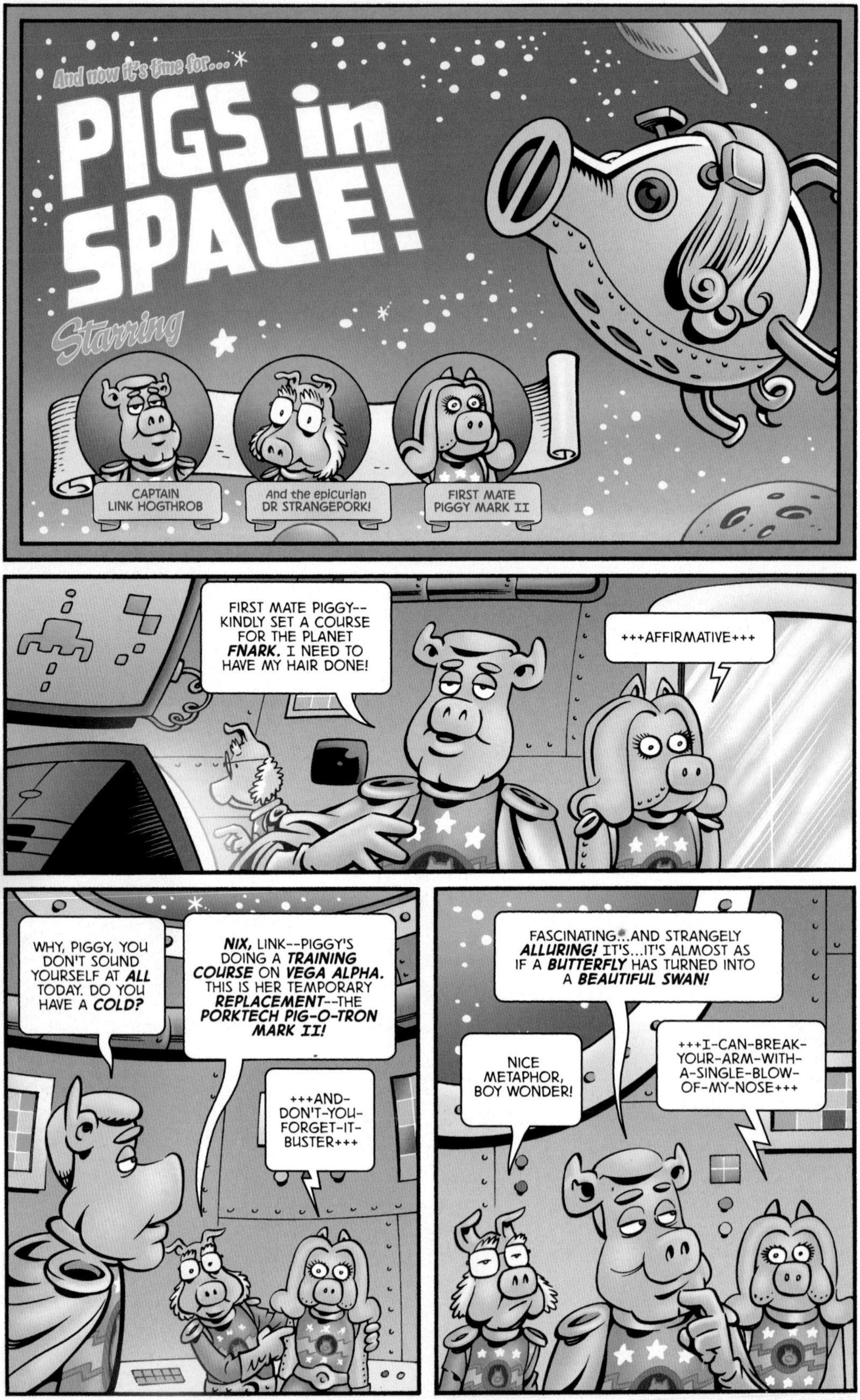
And now it's time for...
PIGS in SPACE!
Starring
CAPTAIN LINK HOGTHROB
And the epicurian DR STRANGEPORK!
FIRST MATE PIGGY MARK II
FIRST MATE PIGGY--KINDLY SET A COURSE FOR THE PLANET FNARK. I NEED TO HAVE MY HAIR DONE!
+++AFFIRMATIVE+++
WHY, PIGGY, YOU DON'T SOUND YOURSELF AT ALL TODAY. DO YOU HAVE A COLD?
NIX, LINK--PIGGY'S DOING A TRAINING COURSE ON VEGA ALPHA. THIS IS HER TEMPORARY REPLACEMENT--THE PORKTECH PIG-O-TRON MARK II!
+++AND-DON'T-YOU-FORGET-IT-BUSTER+++
FASCINATING...AND STRANGELY ALLURING! IT'S...IT'S ALMOST AS IF A BUTTERFLY HAS TURNED INTO A BEAUTIFUL SWAN!
NICE METAPHOR, BOY WONDER!
+++I-CAN-BREAK-YOUR-ARM-WITH-A-SINGLE-BLOW-OF-MY-NOSE+++

GEE, THIS DROID'S ALMOST AS LIPPY AS THE *REAL THING*, DOC! CAN WE CRANK DOWN THE *SARCASM* A NOTCH?

THAT'S THE BEAUTY OF THE *PIG-O-TRON MARK II*, CAPTAIN--EVERYTHING'S *FULLY CUSTOMIZABLE!* LET ME JUST CONSULT THE *MANUAL...*

THWUDD

+++YOU-ARE-A-VERY-UGLY-MAN-CAPTAIN+++

HURRY, DOC--SHE'S *TEASING* ME!

I'M LOOKING, I'M LOOKING! LOTTA PAGES HERE...

AAH, WHAT THE HECK. I'LL TAKE A GUESS AND HIT BUTTON "A". WHAT'S THE *WORST* THAT COULD HAPPEN?

ER...SHE COULD MOBILIZE AN ARMY OF ROBOTS TO TAKE OVER THE UNIVERSE?

YES, BUT APART FROM THAT.

THERE! GOOD AS NEW!

I'LL TRY MY MASCULINE CHARMS! AHEM... PIGGY, DEAREST, MIGHT I HAVE THE HONOR OF YOUR *COMPANY...?*

HIIIIIII-YAAAAA!!!

OW.

OW.

OW.

OR POSSIBLY BUTTON "B".

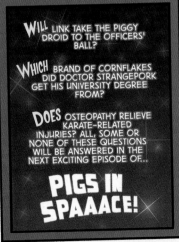

WILL LINK TAKE THE PIGGY DROID TO THE OFFICERS' BALL?

WHICH BRAND OF CORNFLAKES DID DOCTOR STRANGEPORK GET HIS UNIVERSITY DEGREE FROM?

DOES OSTEOPATHY RELIEVE KARATE-RELATED INJURIES? ALL, SOME OR NONE OF THESE QUESTIONS WILL BE ANSWERED IN THE NEXT EXCITING EPISODE OF...

PIGS IN SPAAACE!

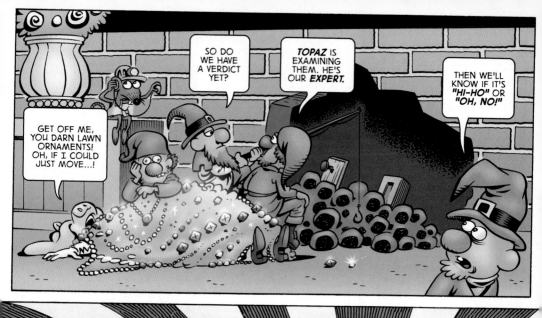

GET OFF ME, YOU DARN LAWN ORNAMENTS! OH, IF I COULD JUST MOVE...!

SO DO WE HAVE A VERDICT YET?

TOPAZ IS EXAMINING THEM. HE'S OUR *EXPERT.*

THEN WE'LL KNOW IF IT'S *"HI-HO"* OR *"OH, NO!"*

TOPAZ! WHAT'S THE GOOD WORD?

I DON'T LIKE THE LOOK ON HIS FACE...

'TWAS IN THE YEAR OF THE GREAT HUNT FOR TREASURE WHEN SOME DWARFS FOUND A PIG COVERED IN STONES, WHICH DID NOT GIVE GREAT PLEASURE! FOR THE STONES WERE MERE FAKES, AS SHABBY AS COULD BE AND I THINK THEY MIGHT WELL HAVE BETTER BEEN LEFT BENEATH A TREE.

YES, SHABBY, I SAY! FOR AS FAKES GO THESE ARE WITHOUT A DOUBT SOME OF THE WORST FAKES I EVER DID KNOW. I HAVE ONLY EVER SEEN WORSE FAKES ON ONE OCCASION, WHEN MRS MACTAVISH DID SHOW ME A NECKLACE MADE ENTIRELY FROM RAISINS.

SO PACK UP YOUR BAGS AND YOUR JEWELLER'S TOOLS FOR EACH AND EVERY ONE OF US HAVE BEEN PLAYED FOR FOOLS! AND LET US NO MORE ALLOW OURSELVES TO BE DISTRACTED BY GAUDY BAUBLES WORN UPON A PIG WHOSE ROLES ARE WITHOUT EXCEPTION TERRIBLY ACTED.

OOOOOOOHHHHHHHH...

UH-OH! HE'S GETTING READY FOR A *POEM!*

HE ONLY GIVES RECITALS WHEN THERE'S BEEN A *TERRIBLE* DISASTER! *BRACE YOURSELVES, MEN!*

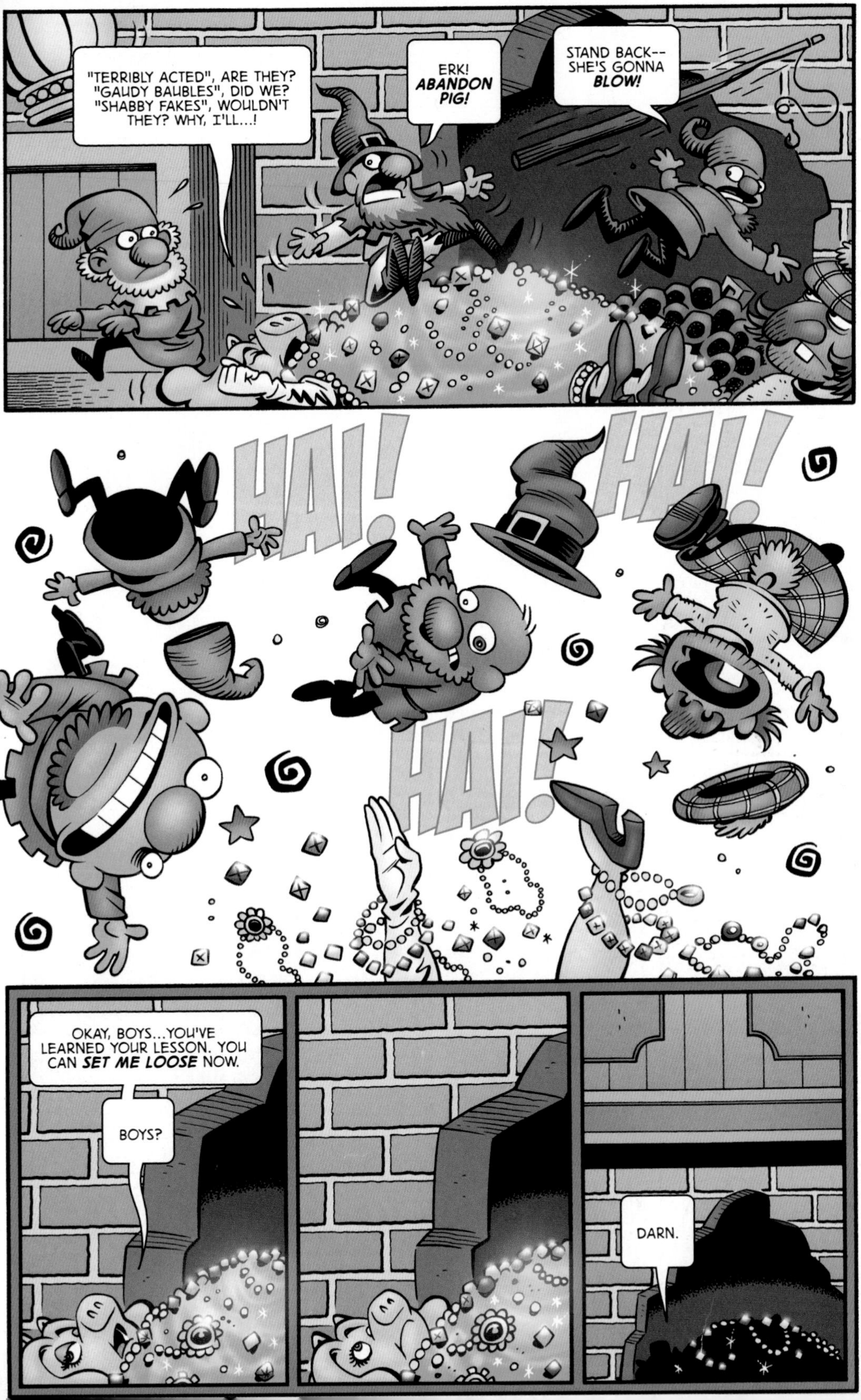
"TERRIBLY ACTED", ARE THEY? "GAUDY BAUBLES", DID WE? "SHABBY FAKES", WOULDN'T THEY? WHY, I'LL...!
ERK! ABANDON PIG!
STAND BACK-- SHE'S GONNA BLOW!
HAI!
HAI!
HAI!
OKAY, BOYS...YOU'VE LEARNED YOUR LESSON. YOU CAN SET ME LOOSE NOW.
BOYS?
DARN.

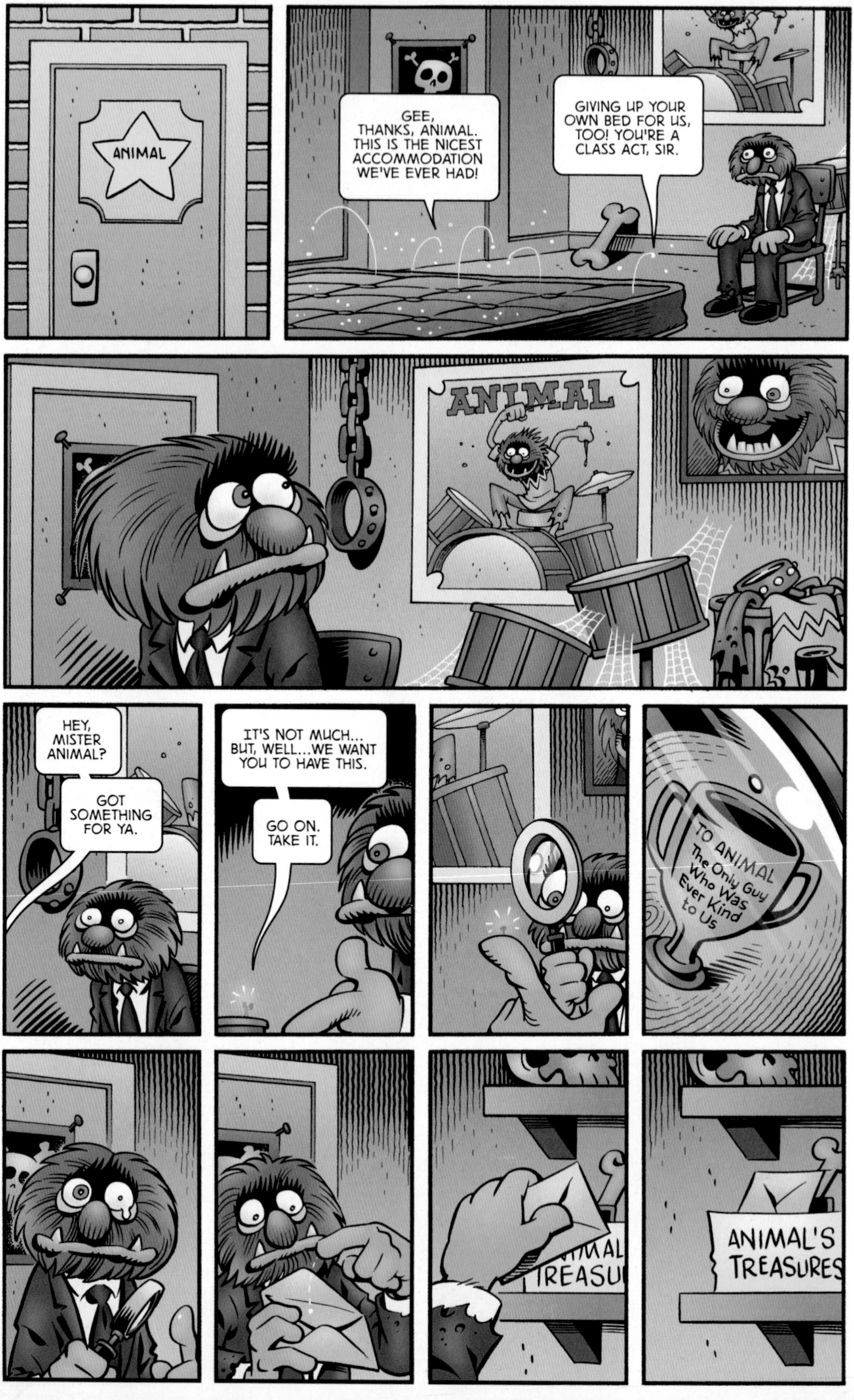
ANIMAL
GEE, THANKS, ANIMAL. THIS IS THE NICEST ACCOMMODATION WE'VE EVER HAD!
GIVING UP YOUR OWN BED FOR US, TOO! YOU'RE A CLASS ACT, SIR.
ANIMAL
HEY, MISTER ANIMAL?
GOT SOMETHING FOR YA.
IT'S NOT MUCH... BUT, WELL...WE WANT YOU TO HAVE THIS.
GO ON. TAKE IT.
TO ANIMAL The Only Guy Who Was Ever Kind to Us
ANIMAL'S TREASURES

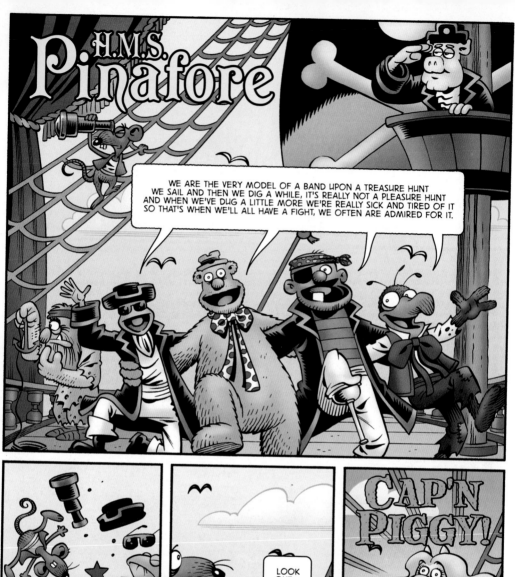

H.M.S. Pinafore

WE ARE THE VERY MODEL OF A BAND UPON A TREASURE HUNT
WE SAIL AND THEN WE DIG A WHILE, IT'S REALLY NOT A PLEASURE HUNT
AND WHEN WE'VE DUG A LITTLE MORE WE'RE REALLY SICK AND TIRED OF IT
SO THAT'S WHEN WE'LL ALL HAVE A FIGHT, WE OFTEN ARE ADMIRED FOR IT.

LOOK OUT-- IT'S...

CAP'N PIGGY!

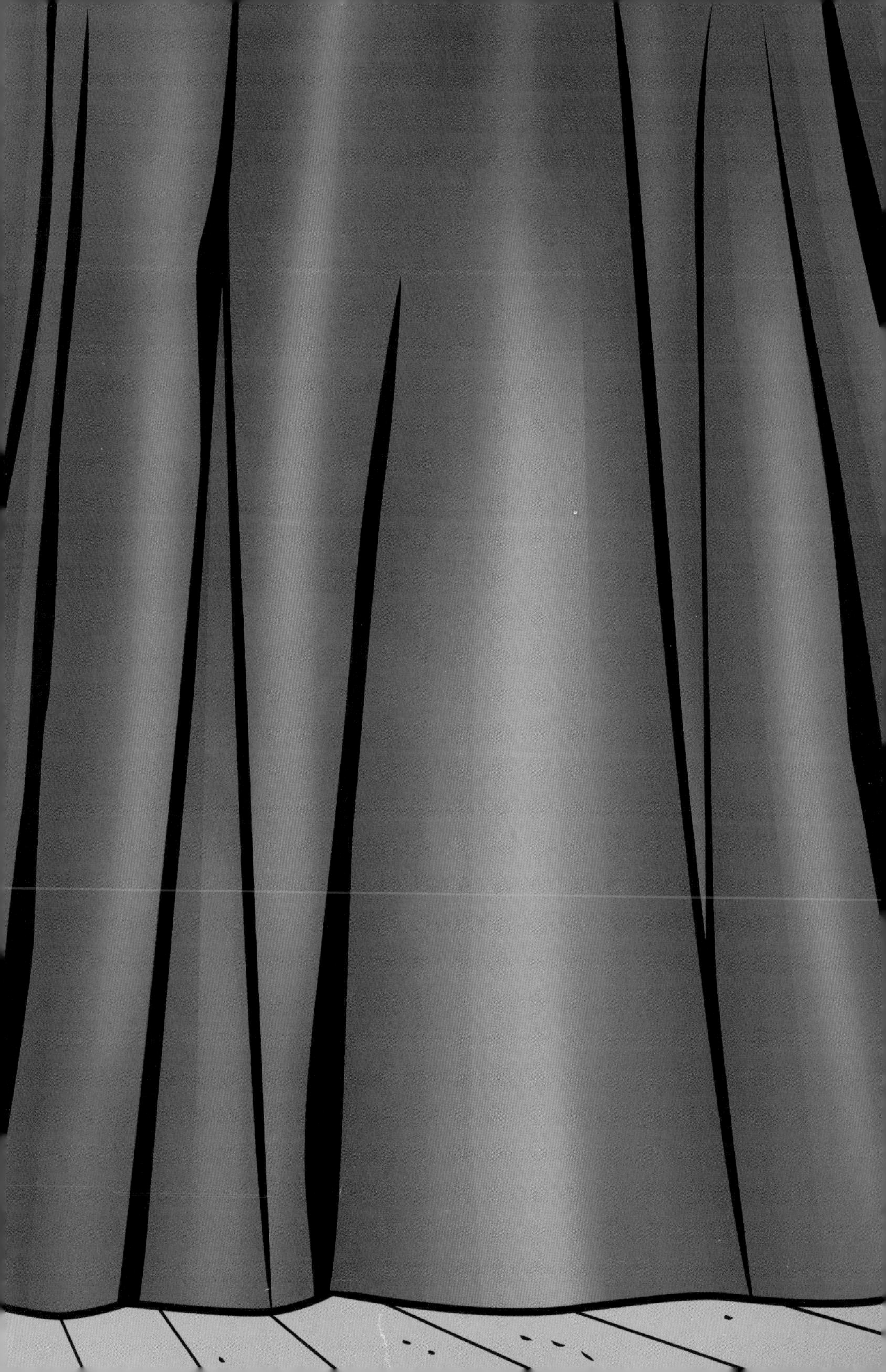

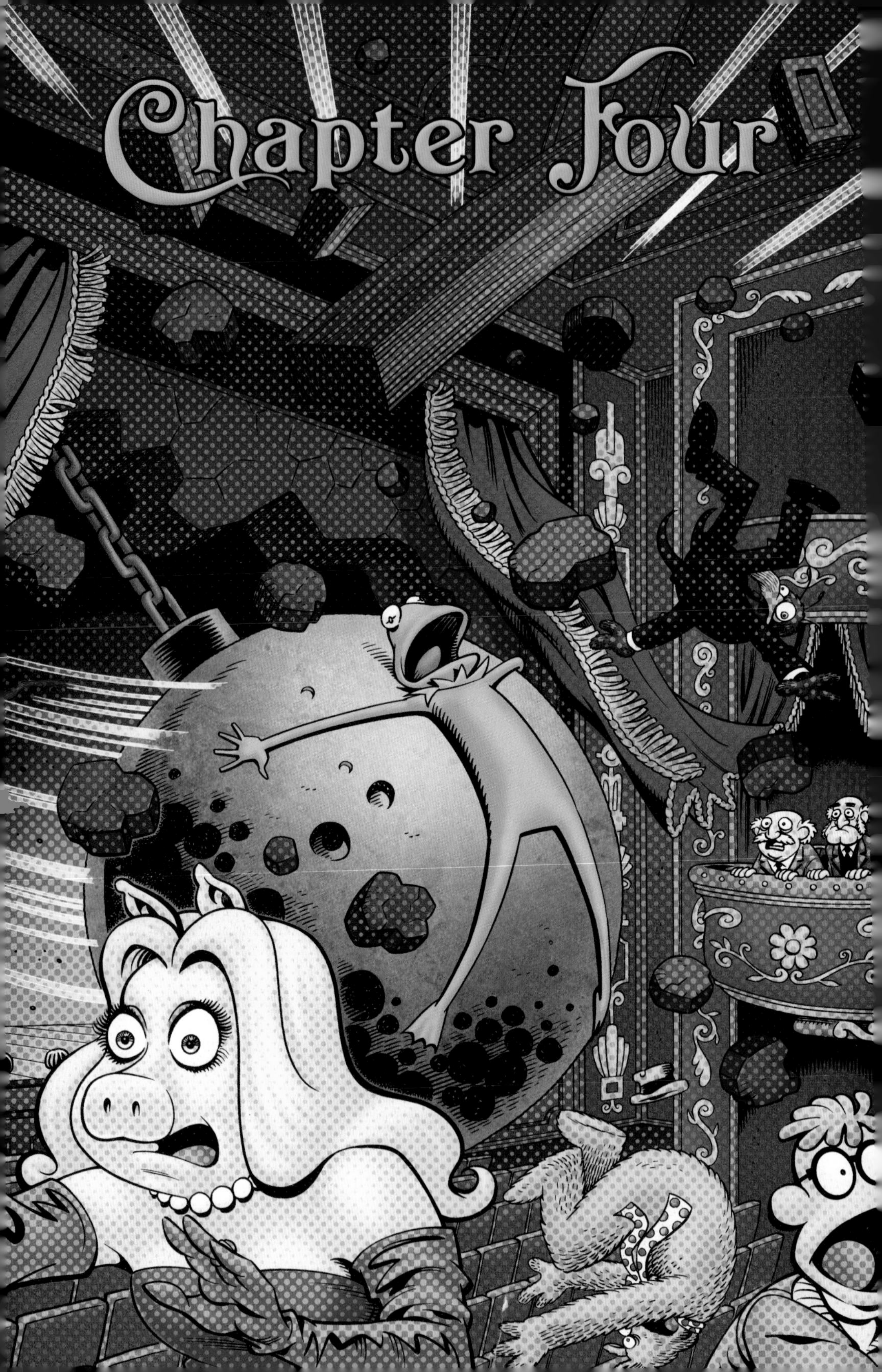
Chapter Four

ALL RIGHT, BROTHERS AND SISTERS--LET'S CALL THIS MEETING TO *ORDER!*

AS YOU KNOW, SCOOTER DISCOVERED A MAP TELLING US THAT TREASURE IS HIDDEN *SOMEWHERE* IN THIS BUILDING-- BUT, EHH, IT WAS A BIT *VAGUE* ABOUT THE *DETAILS.*

HEY, BROTHER RIZZO!

GET OFF!

DETAILS SHMETAILS!

SHH! *HEAR ME OUT!* HOWZABOUT, INSTEAD OF TRIPPIN' OVER EACH OTHER, WE *COORDINATE* OUR EFFORTS?

THEN, WHEN WE FIND THE *LOOT,* WE SPLIT *YOUR* CUT *EVEN-STEVENS,* SO *EVERYONE* GETS A PIECE!

SOUNDS -- *HEY!* "*OUR* CUT"?

SO WHAT'S *YOUR* CUT?

YEAH! THIS SOUNDS *FISHY* TO ME!

NAWWW, IT'S SIMPLE. I MERELY SPLIT THE DIFFERENTIAL OF THE SQUARE ON THE HYPOTENUSE, THEREBY ASSIGNING MYSELF A PROPORTIONAL AMOUNT IN DIRECT INVERSE RATIO TO MY CONTRIBUTIONS AS *CHIEF POO-BAH, EVENTS CO-ORDINATOR.* ANY QUESTIONS? GOOD.

$$\triangle \cdots \bigcirc \sqrt[\circ]{3}$$
$$=> 5e \%$$
$$\pi \times \emptyset \uparrow \frac{32}{15}($$
$$= 485e < 32y$$

I TRUST RIZZO-- HE *LOOKS OUT* FOR US RATS. I'M SIGNIN' UP.

ME, TOO. HE WOULDN'T DO WRONG BY US.

NOT UNLESS HE COULD GET AWAY WITH IT.

MAYBE *RIZZO* WOULDN'T...BUT *KISMET THE TOAD* CERTAINLY WOULD! OH, TREASURE-- COME TO *PAPA...!*

ALL VERY INTERESTING... BUT ISN'T SOMEONE GOING TO MENTION ANIMAL'S *JEKYLL AND HYDE* PROBLEM, MISS PIGGY'S JEWELS TURNING OUT TO BE *FAKES* AND THOSE WEIRD *GERANIUMS* DOCTOR HONEYDEW IS GROWING?

WHAT, AND MAKE THIS COMIC COMPREHENSIBLE? YOU'RE *NEW* HERE, AREN'T YOU?

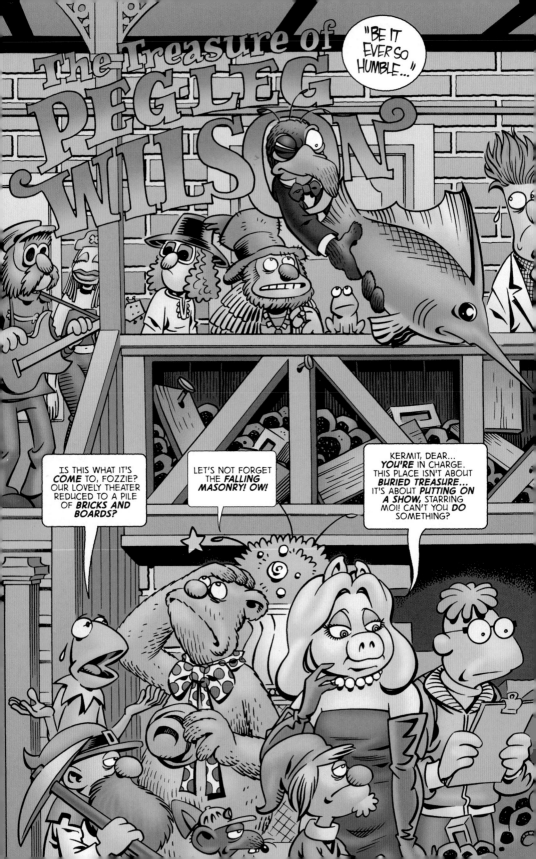

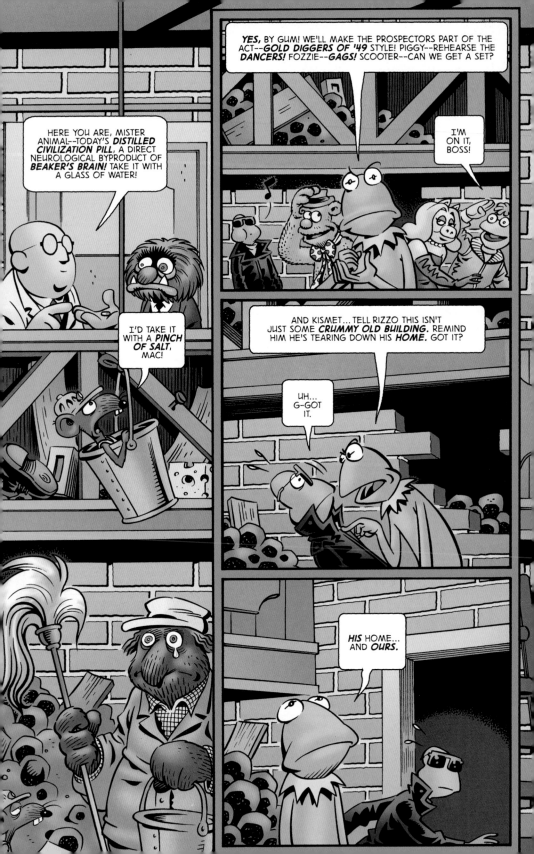

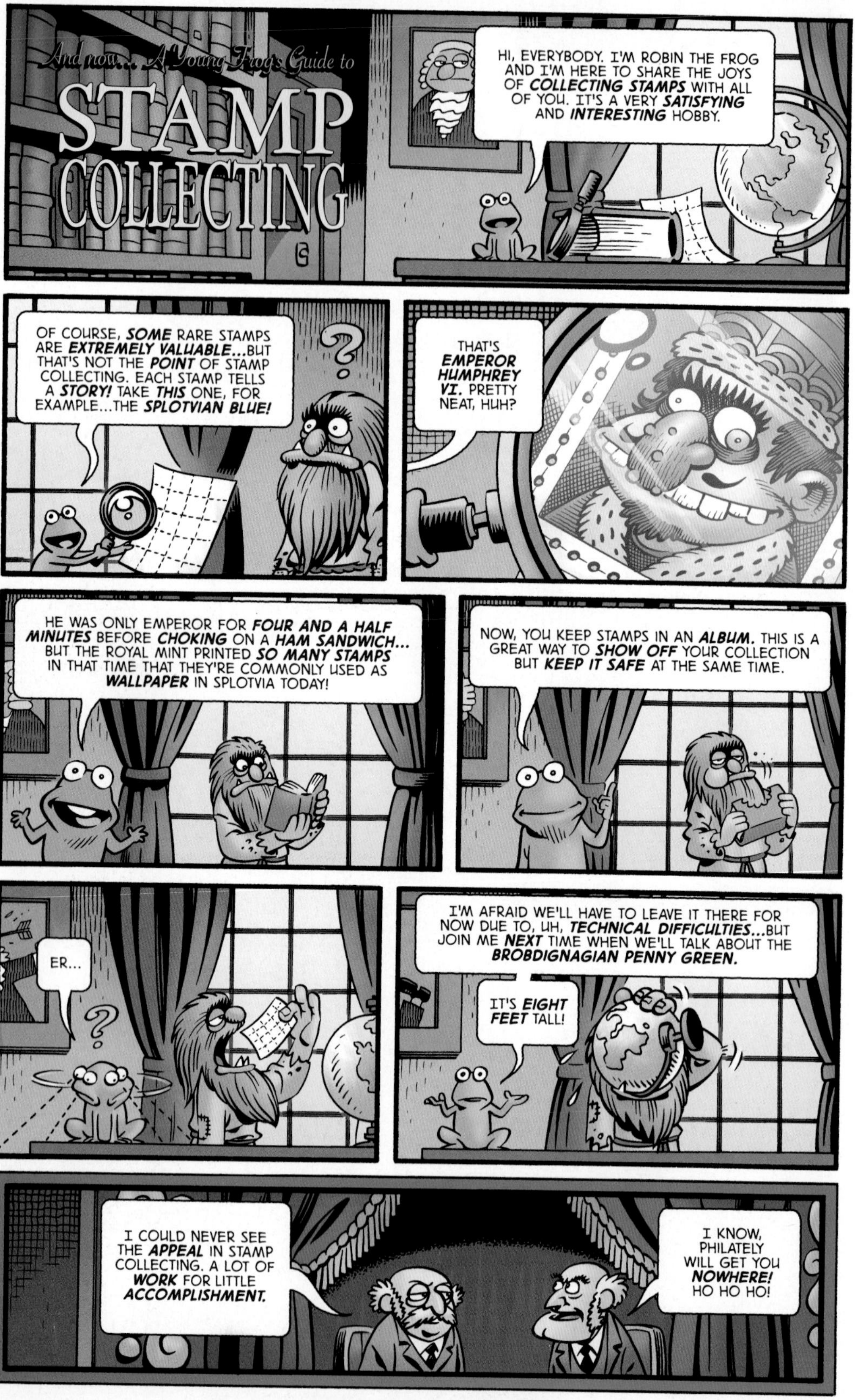
And now... A Young Frog's Guide to
STAMP COLLECTING
HI, EVERYBODY. I'M ROBIN THE FROG AND I'M HERE TO SHARE THE JOYS OF COLLECTING STAMPS WITH ALL OF YOU. IT'S A VERY SATISFYING AND INTERESTING HOBBY.
OF COURSE, SOME RARE STAMPS ARE EXTREMELY VALUABLE...BUT THAT'S NOT THE POINT OF STAMP COLLECTING. EACH STAMP TELLS A STORY! TAKE THIS ONE, FOR EXAMPLE...THE SPLOTVIAN BLUE!
?
THAT'S EMPEROR HUMPHREY VI. PRETTY NEAT, HUH?
HE WAS ONLY EMPEROR FOR FOUR AND A HALF MINUTES BEFORE CHOKING ON A HAM SANDWICH... BUT THE ROYAL MINT PRINTED SO MANY STAMPS IN THAT TIME THAT THEY'RE COMMONLY USED AS WALLPAPER IN SPLOTVIA TODAY!
NOW, YOU KEEP STAMPS IN AN ALBUM. THIS IS A GREAT WAY TO SHOW OFF YOUR COLLECTION BUT KEEP IT SAFE AT THE SAME TIME.
ER...
?
I'M AFRAID WE'LL HAVE TO LEAVE IT THERE FOR NOW DUE TO, UH, TECHNICAL DIFFICULTIES...BUT JOIN ME NEXT TIME WHEN WE'LL TALK ABOUT THE BROBDIGNAGIAN PENNY GREEN.
IT'S EIGHT FEET TALL!
I COULD NEVER SEE THE APPEAL IN STAMP COLLECTING. A LOT OF WORK FOR LITTLE ACCOMPLISHMENT.
I KNOW, PHILATELY WILL GET YOU NOWHERE! HO HO HO!

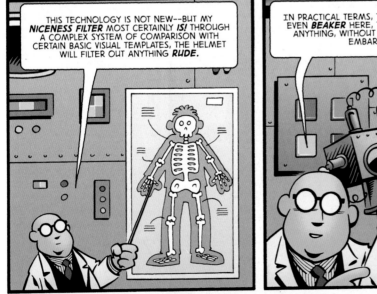

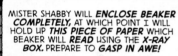

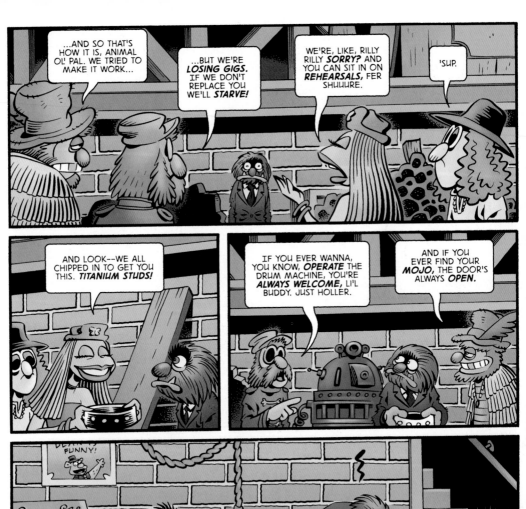

REMEMBER, MY BOY--YOU CAN *STOP* TAKING THE DISTILLED CIVILIZATION PILLS AT *ANY TIME!*

NNAAAARGHH!!

PITTER PITTER PITTER PITT

PITTER PITTER PITTER PITTE!

DRUMS.

CRR-RAAKKK!!

DRUUMMMSSS!!!

PITTERPITTERPITTERPITTERPITT

D-DRUUUMMMSSS....

PITTER

PITTERPITTERPITTERPITTERPITTE

DRUMS! DRUMS! *DRUMS!*

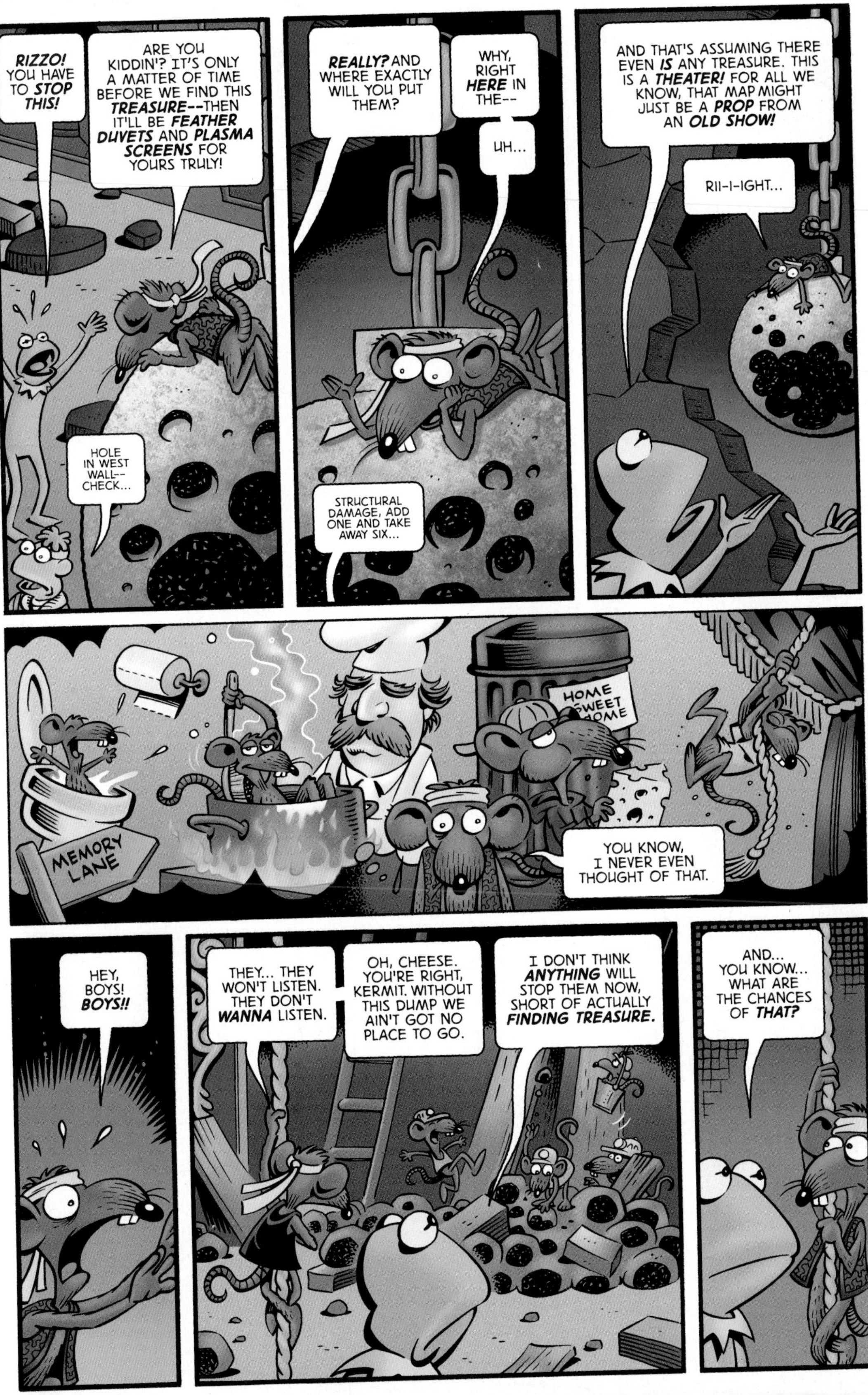
RIZZO! YOU HAVE TO STOP THIS!
ARE YOU KIDDIN'? IT'S ONLY A MATTER OF TIME BEFORE WE FIND THIS TREASURE--THEN IT'LL BE FEATHER DUVETS AND PLASMA SCREENS FOR YOURS TRULY!
HOLE IN WEST WALL--CHECK...
REALLY? AND WHERE EXACTLY WILL YOU PUT THEM?
WHY, RIGHT HERE IN THE--
UH...
STRUCTURAL DAMAGE, ADD ONE AND TAKE AWAY SIX...
AND THAT'S ASSUMING THERE EVEN IS ANY TREASURE. THIS IS A THEATER! FOR ALL WE KNOW, THAT MAP MIGHT JUST BE A PROP FROM AN OLD SHOW!
RII-I-IGHT...
HOME SWEET HOME
MEMORY LANE
YOU KNOW, I NEVER EVEN THOUGHT OF THAT.
HEY, BOYS! BOYS!!
THEY... THEY WON'T LISTEN. THEY DON'T WANNA LISTEN.
OH, CHEESE. YOU'RE RIGHT, KERMIT. WITHOUT THIS DUMP WE AIN'T GOT NO PLACE TO GO.
I DON'T THINK ANYTHING WILL STOP THEM NOW, SHORT OF ACTUALLY FINDING TREASURE.
AND... YOU KNOW... WHAT ARE THE CHANCES OF THAT?

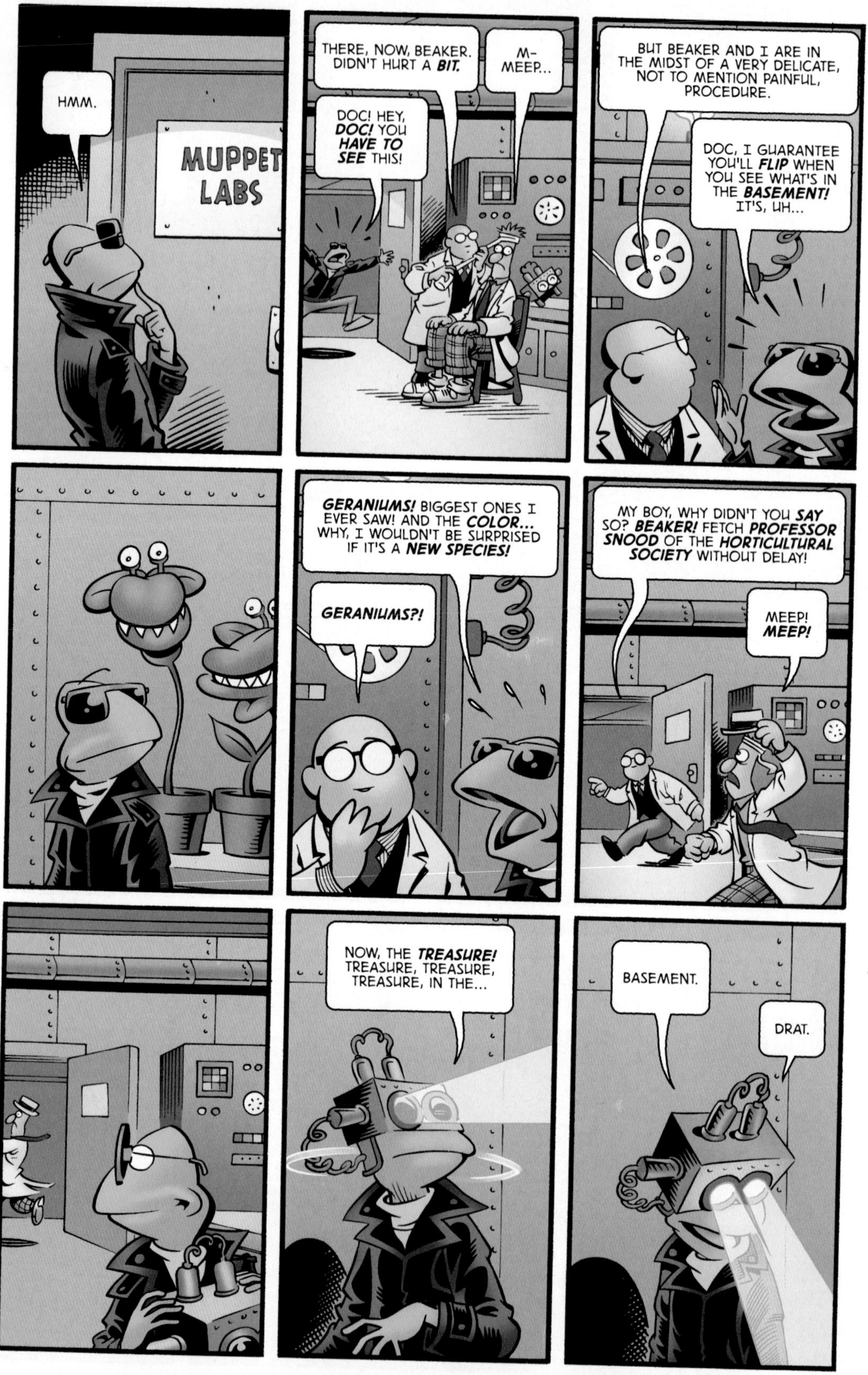
HMM.
MUPPET LABS
THERE, NOW, BEAKER. DIDN'T HURT A **BIT.**
M-MEEP...
DOC! HEY, **DOC!** YOU **HAVE TO SEE** THIS!
BUT BEAKER AND I ARE IN THE MIDST OF A VERY DELICATE, NOT TO MENTION PAINFUL, PROCEDURE.
DOC, I GUARANTEE YOU'LL **FLIP** WHEN YOU SEE WHAT'S IN THE **BASEMENT!** IT'S, UH...
GERANIUMS! BIGGEST ONES I EVER SAW! AND THE **COLOR...** WHY, I WOULDN'T BE SURPRISED IF IT'S A **NEW SPECIES!**
GERANIUMS?!
MY BOY, WHY DIDN'T YOU **SAY** SO? **BEAKER!** FETCH **PROFESSOR SNOOD** OF THE **HORTICULTURAL SOCIETY** WITHOUT DELAY!
MEEP! **MEEP!**
NOW, THE **TREASURE!** TREASURE, TREASURE, TREASURE, IN THE...
BASEMENT.
DRAT.

DEAR ME. WHAT SORT OF GERANIUM COULD POSSIBLY THRIVE IN *PITCH BLACKNESS?* PERHAPS THERE'S BEEN A *MISTAKE*...

THERE WE GO!

GOODNESS--THIS *CAN'T* BE RIGHT. I SMELL A *RAT*.

THWAK

RATS HAD NOTHING TO DO WITH IT.

TREASURE, ON THE OTHER HAND ⋟NNNGGHH!⋞ HAS EVERYTHING TO DO WITH *EVERYTHING!*

OOOH, BABY! *THE TREASURE OF PEG-LEG WILSON*--AT *LAST!* AND IT'S MINE, *AAALLLL* MINE! *MWAHAHAHAHAAA!*

THAT'S THE MAN, OFFICER! *ARREST HIM!*

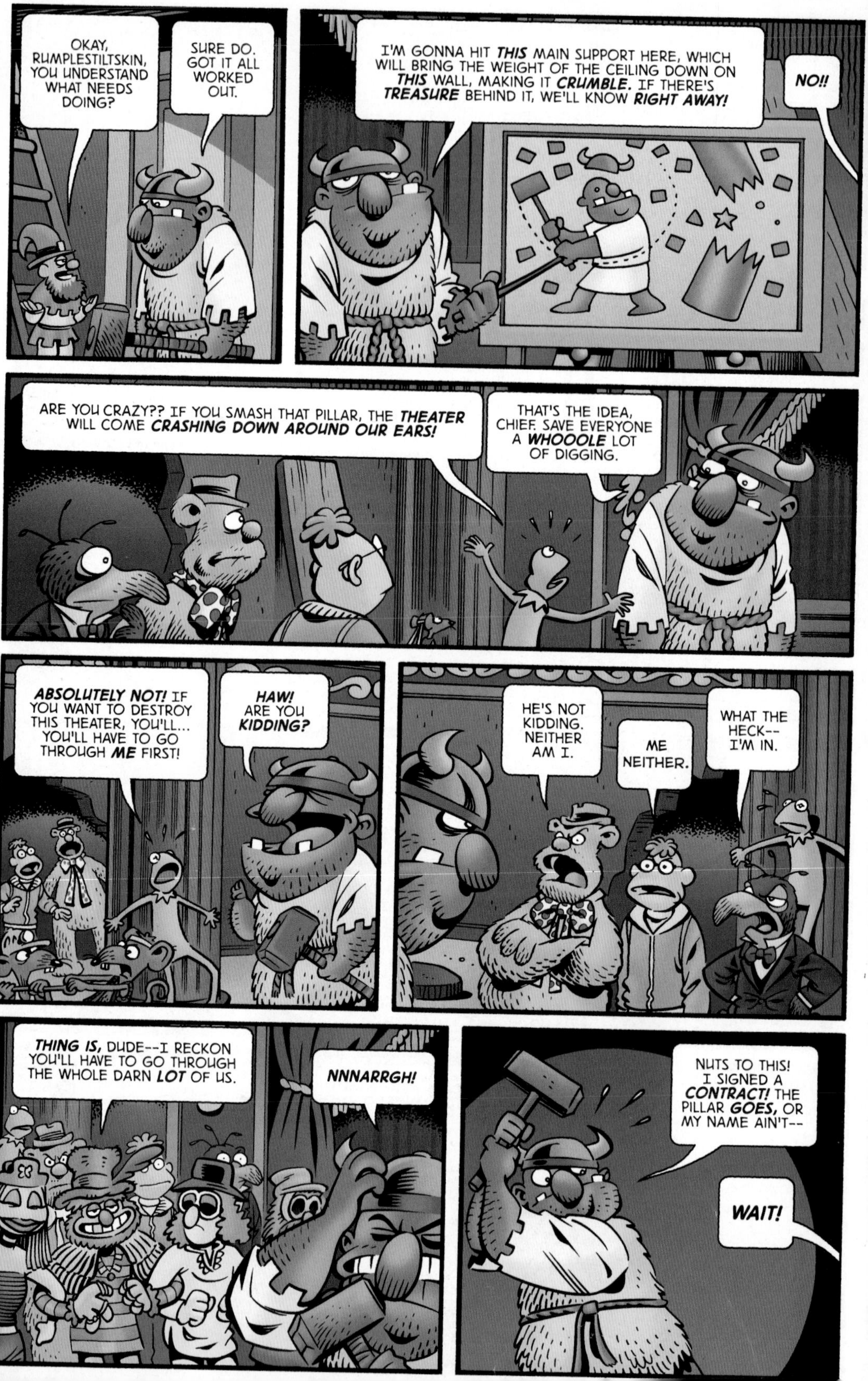
OKAY, RUMPLESTILTSKIN, YOU UNDERSTAND WHAT NEEDS DOING?
SURE DO. GOT IT ALL WORKED OUT.
I'M GONNA HIT THIS MAIN SUPPORT HERE, WHICH WILL BRING THE WEIGHT OF THE CEILING DOWN ON THIS WALL, MAKING IT CRUMBLE. IF THERE'S TREASURE BEHIND IT, WE'LL KNOW RIGHT AWAY!
NO!!
ARE YOU CRAZY?? IF YOU SMASH THAT PILLAR, THE THEATER WILL COME CRASHING DOWN AROUND OUR EARS!
THAT'S THE IDEA, CHIEF. SAVE EVERYONE A WHOOOLE LOT OF DIGGING.
ABSOLUTELY NOT! IF YOU WANT TO DESTROY THIS THEATER, YOU'LL... YOU'LL HAVE TO GO THROUGH ME FIRST!
HAW! ARE YOU KIDDING?
HE'S NOT KIDDING. NEITHER AM I.
ME NEITHER.
WHAT THE HECK-- I'M IN.
THING IS, DUDE--I RECKON YOU'LL HAVE TO GO THROUGH THE WHOLE DARN LOT OF US.
NNNARRGH!
NUTS TO THIS! I SIGNED A CONTRACT! THE PILLAR GOES, OR MY NAME AIN'T--
WAIT!

COOL YOUR ENGINES, BOYS--*WE FOUND THE TREASURE!*

PIGGY! I COULD *KISS* YOU!

REQUEST *NOTED,* CASANOVA.

WHAT IN THE HOOTIN' HECK--?

HAW! IN YOUR *FACE,* UGLY! YOU ARE *SO* FIRED!

YOU'RE *ALL* FIRED! GO! AND *DO* LET THE DOOR HIT YOU ON THE *WAY OUT!*

YOU KNOW, IF I'D WORKED HARDER ON THE LYRICS OF THAT *HI HO* SONG I WROTE, YOU'D BE LOOKING TODAY AT A *RICHER, TALLER* MAN.

TALLER?

YEAH-- I'D FIX MY *FLAT FEET.*

I THINK WE CAN *OPEN THAT CHEST* NOW AND FINALLY FIND OUT WHAT ALL THE *FUSS* WAS ABOUT.

I'M *ON* IT! ⇒NNNGGHHH⇐

DRUUUMMS!!

BOOM! BOOM! BOOM!

HOLY MOLEY! WHAT'S *THAT?*

I *DUNNO,* MAN...BUT IT SOUNDS LIKE...

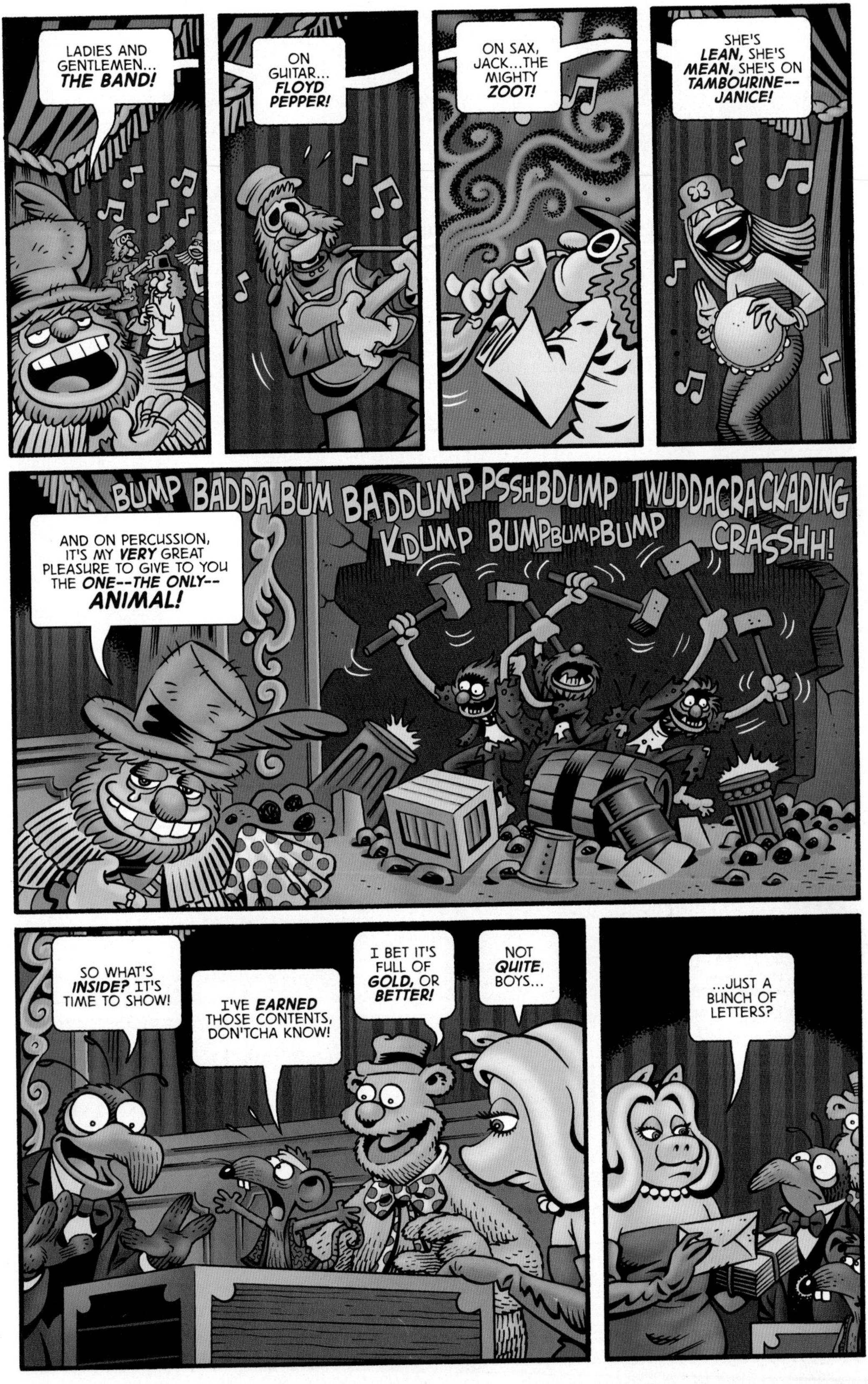
LADIES AND GENTLEMEN... THE BAND!
ON GUITAR... FLOYD PEPPER!
ON SAX, JACK...THE MIGHTY ZOOT!
SHE'S LEAN, SHE'S MEAN, SHE'S ON TAMBOURINE--JANICE!
BUMP BADDA BUM BADDUMP PSSHBDUMP TWUDDACRACKADING
KDUMP BUMPBUMPBUMP
CRASSHH!
AND ON PERCUSSION, IT'S MY VERY GREAT PLEASURE TO GIVE TO YOU THE ONE--THE ONLY--ANIMAL!
SO WHAT'S INSIDE? IT'S TIME TO SHOW!
I'VE EARNED THOSE CONTENTS, DON'TCHA KNOW!
I BET IT'S FULL OF GOLD, OR BETTER!
NOT QUITE, BOYS...
...JUST A BUNCH OF LETTERS?

...AND HERE'S YOUR FIRST PAYMENT FOR REPAIRING THE THEATER. WE'LL BE BACK TO PAY THE REST WHEN YOU'RE DONE.

GEE--WHO'D HAVE GUESSED THAT PEG-LEG WILSON'S STAMPS WOULD BE WORTH SO MUCH MONEY?

WHO'D HAVE GUESSED THAT IT WOULD BE EXACTLY HOW MUCH WE NEED TO FIX THE THEATER?

WHO'D HAVE GUESSED THAT THE DAMAGE CAUSED IN THE LAST FIVE MINUTES OF THE SHOW WOULD DOUBLE THE REPAIR BILL?

SO... WHAT DO WE DO NOW? THE THEATER WON'T BE READY FOR A WHILE.

YOU KNOW, I'VE BEEN THINKING WE SHOULD GO ON TOUR.

OH, KERMIE! C'EST MERVEILLEUX! TO THINK--WE SHALL TREAD THE BOARDS IN EVERY TOWN IN THE LAND!

"EVERY TOWN" MEANING FOUR, BUT THAT'S THE IDEA. THIS IS THE ONLY WAY WE CAN KEEP EARNING WHILE THE OLD PLACE IS SHUT DOWN.

AND WHO KNOWS? WE MIGHT BE WALKING ON THE VERY SAME STAGE WHERE PEG-LEG WILSON WAS SHOT OUT OF A CANNON THREE TIMES A DAY.

YEAH!

ALL ABOARD, EVERYBODY!

THIS IS GONNA BE GREAT--DOING IT OLD-SCHOOL!

YEAH-- FOR OLD-SCHOOL WAGES!

YOU MEAN WE ACTUALLY GET PAID?

SUCH A SHAME ABOUT THE GERANIUMS. I DO HOPE BEAKER DIDN'T GET LOST...

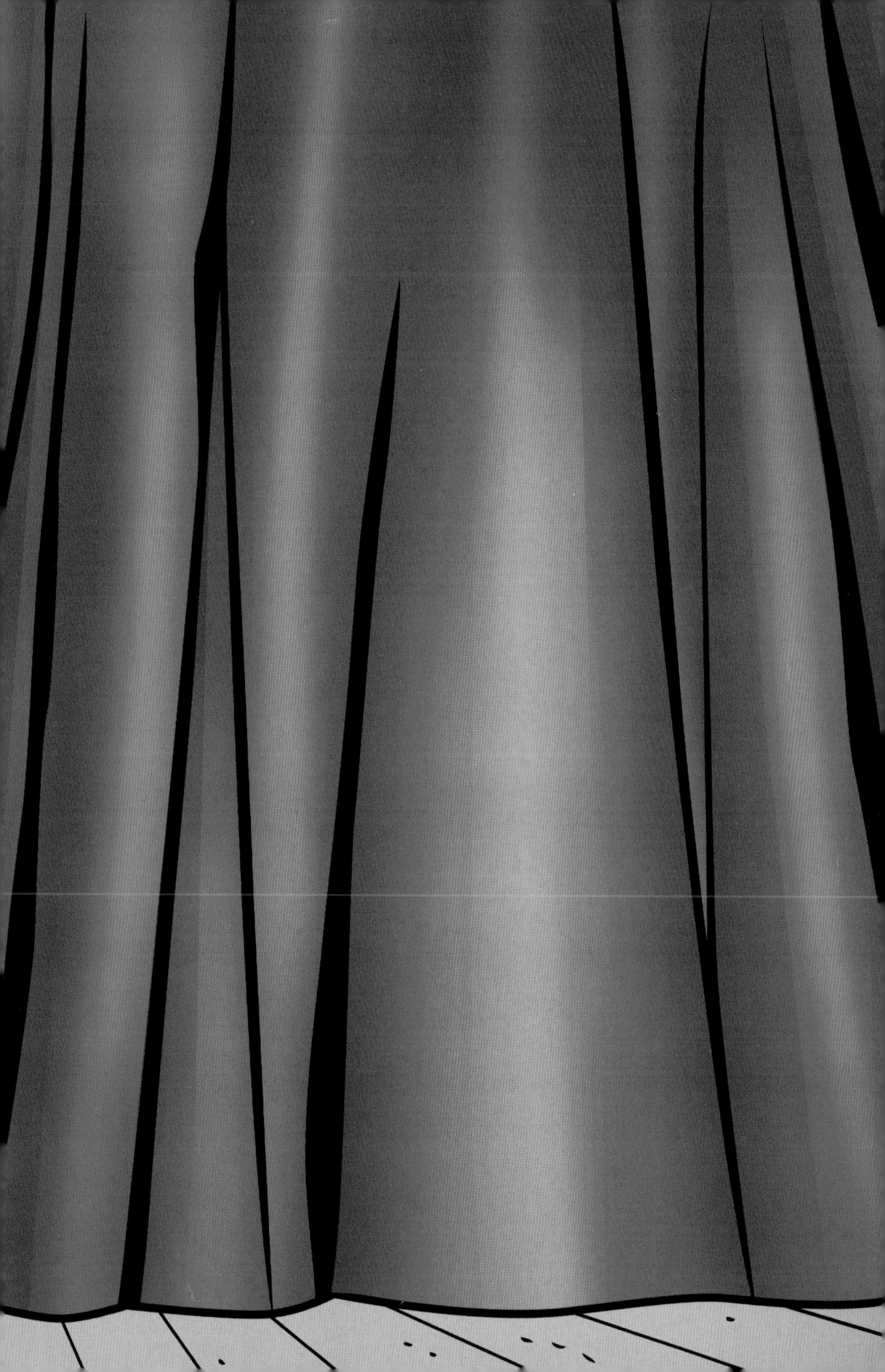

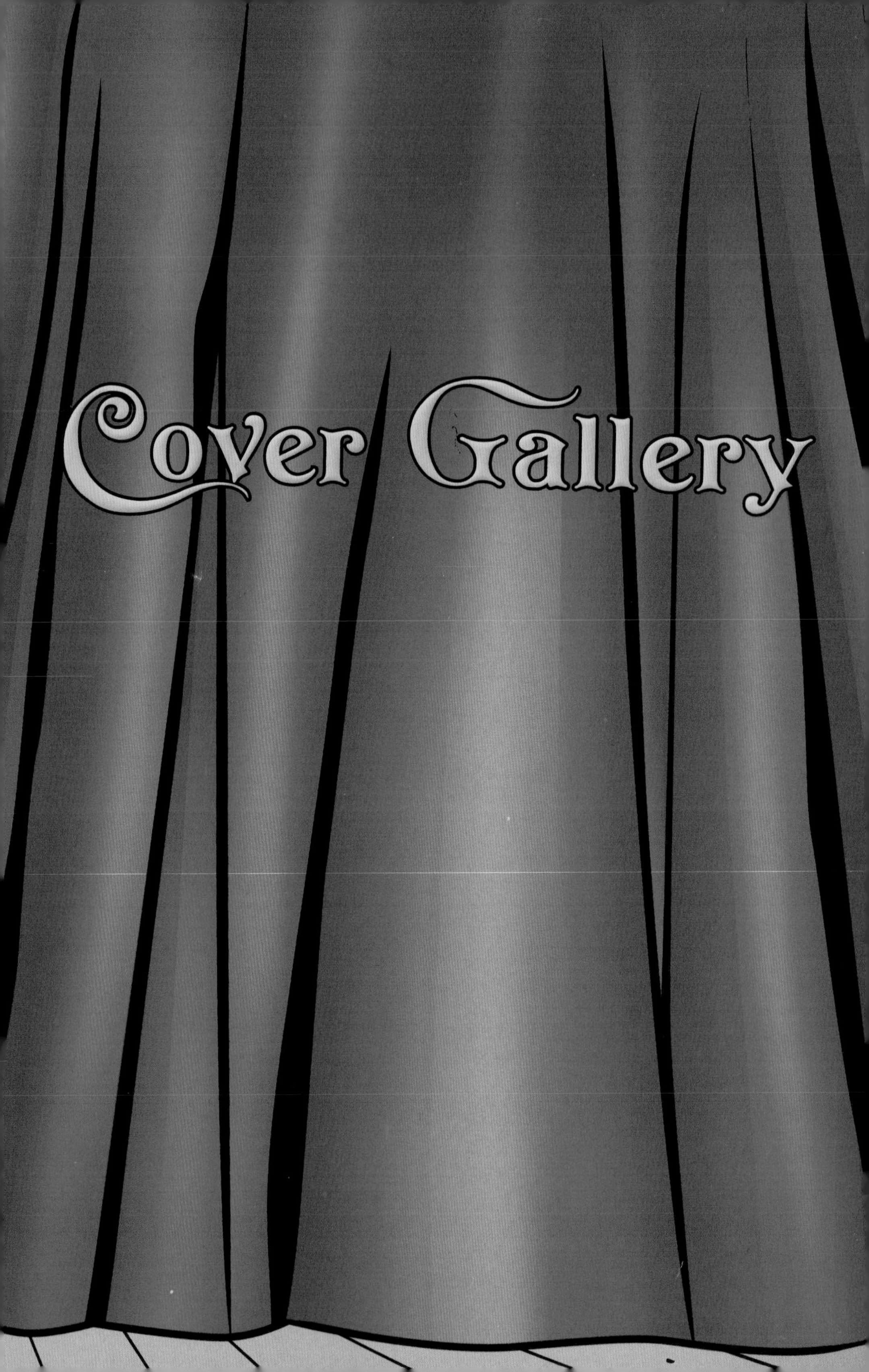
Cover Gallery

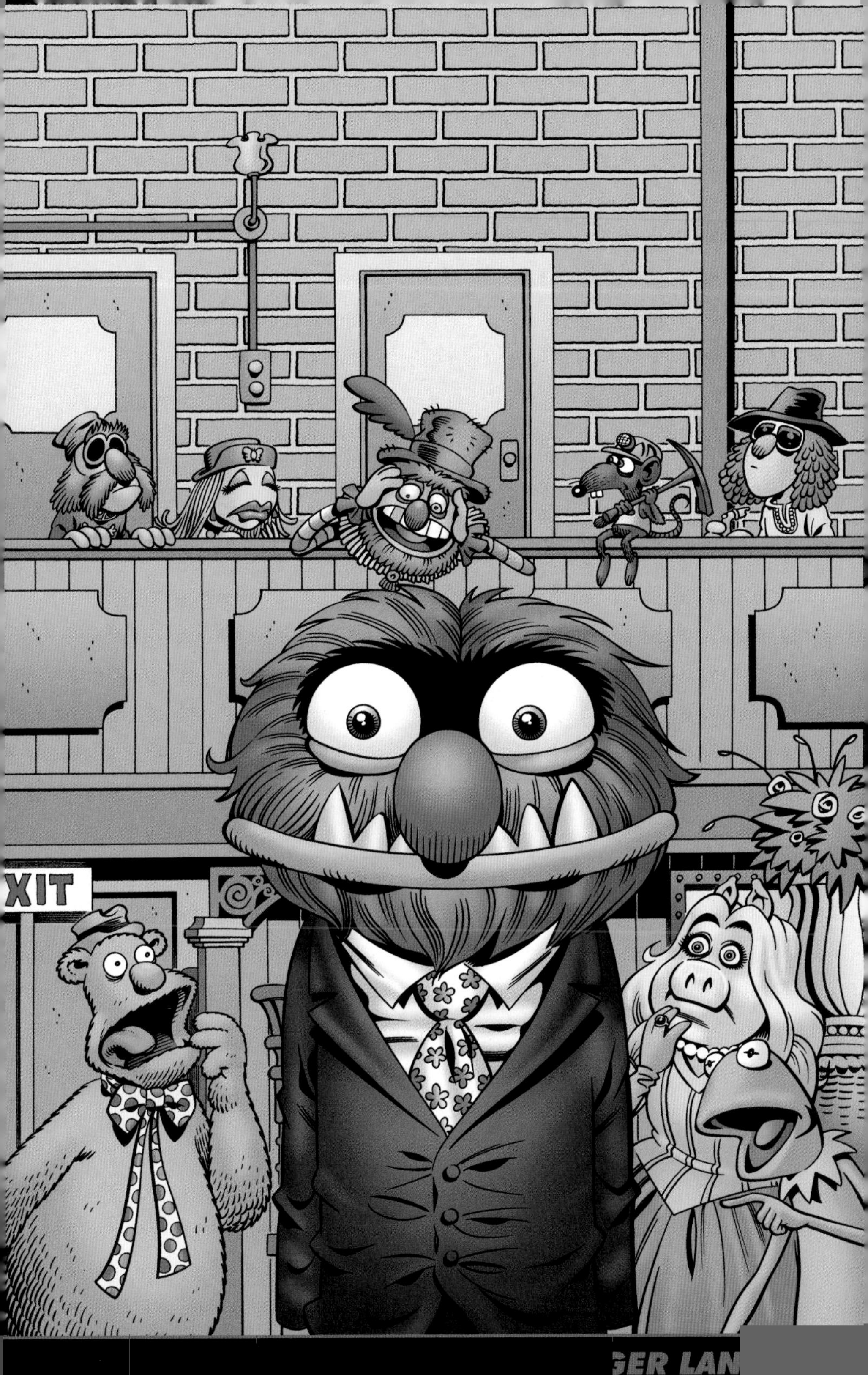
XIT
GER LAN

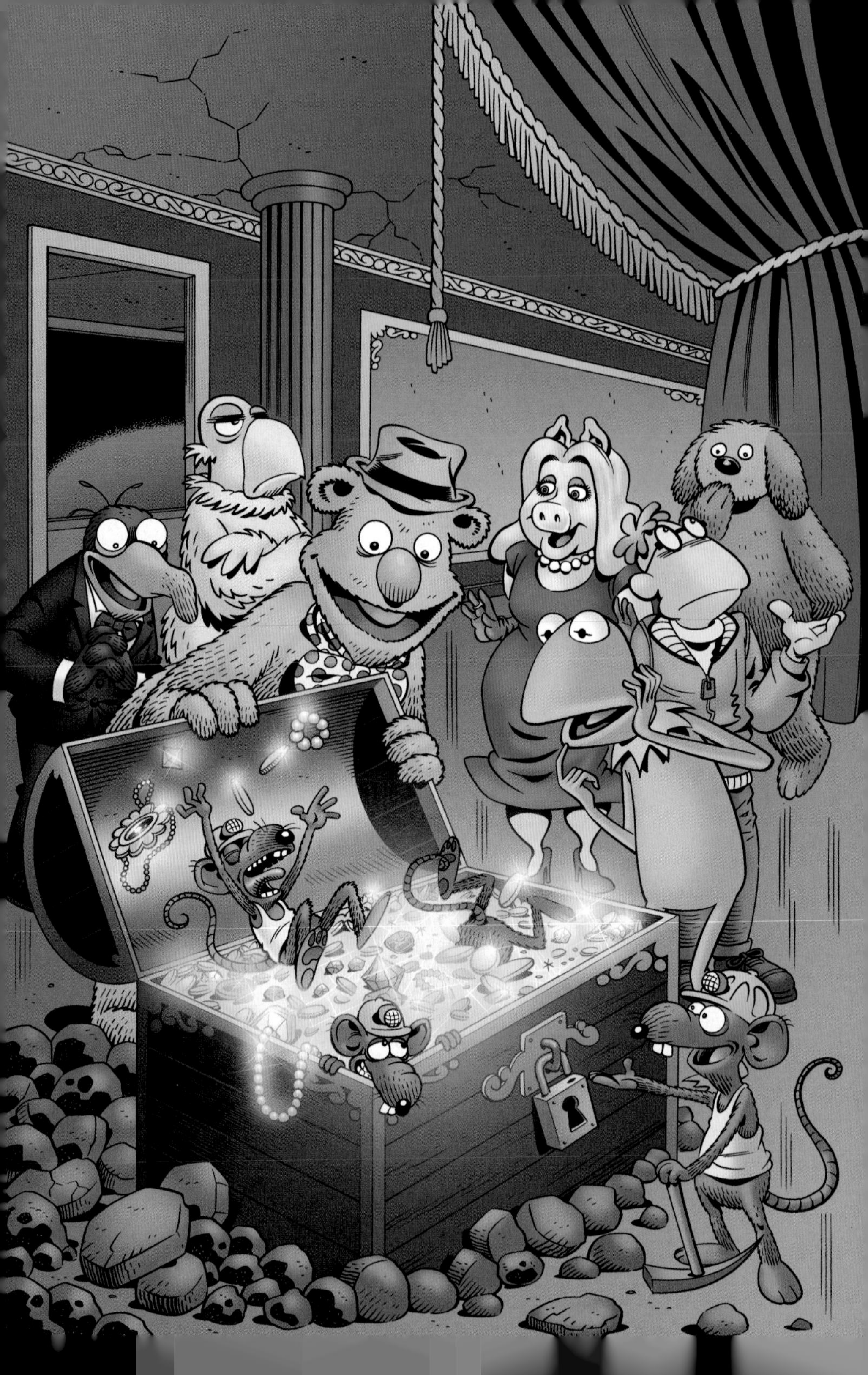

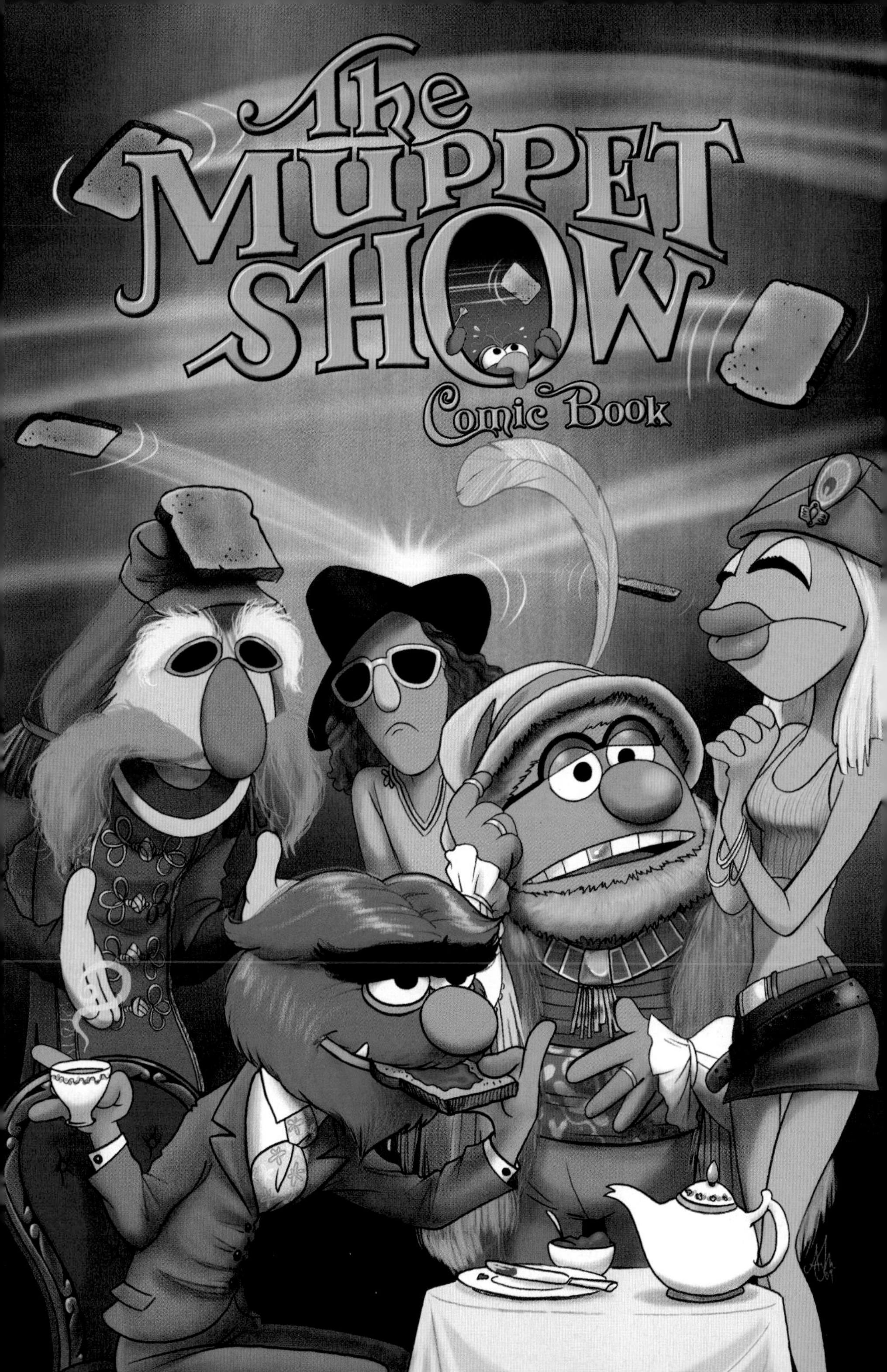
The
MUPPET
SHOW
Comic Book

ULTIMATE COMICS EXCLUSIVE: AMY MEBBERSON

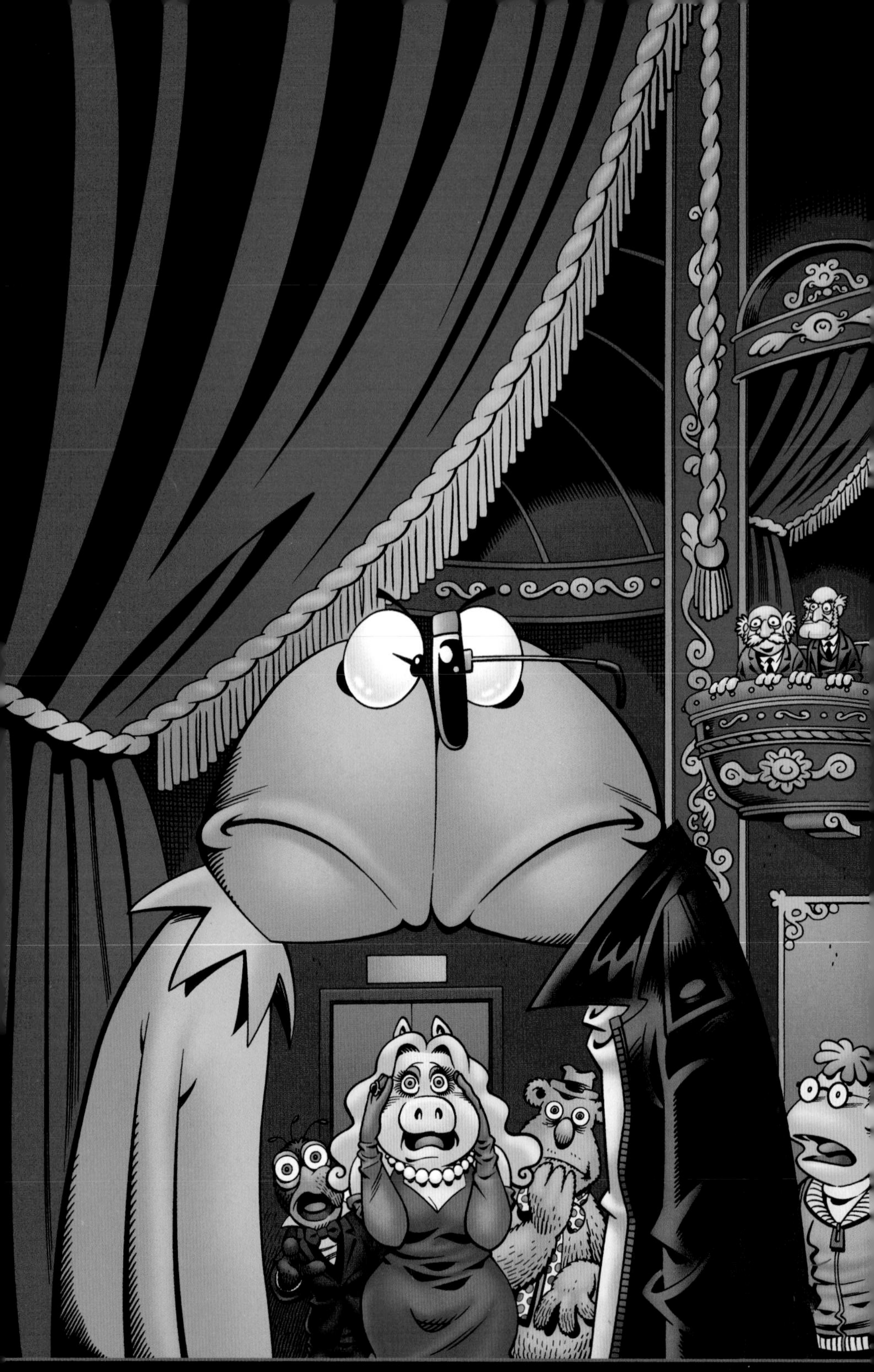

COVER 24: ROGER LANGRIDGE

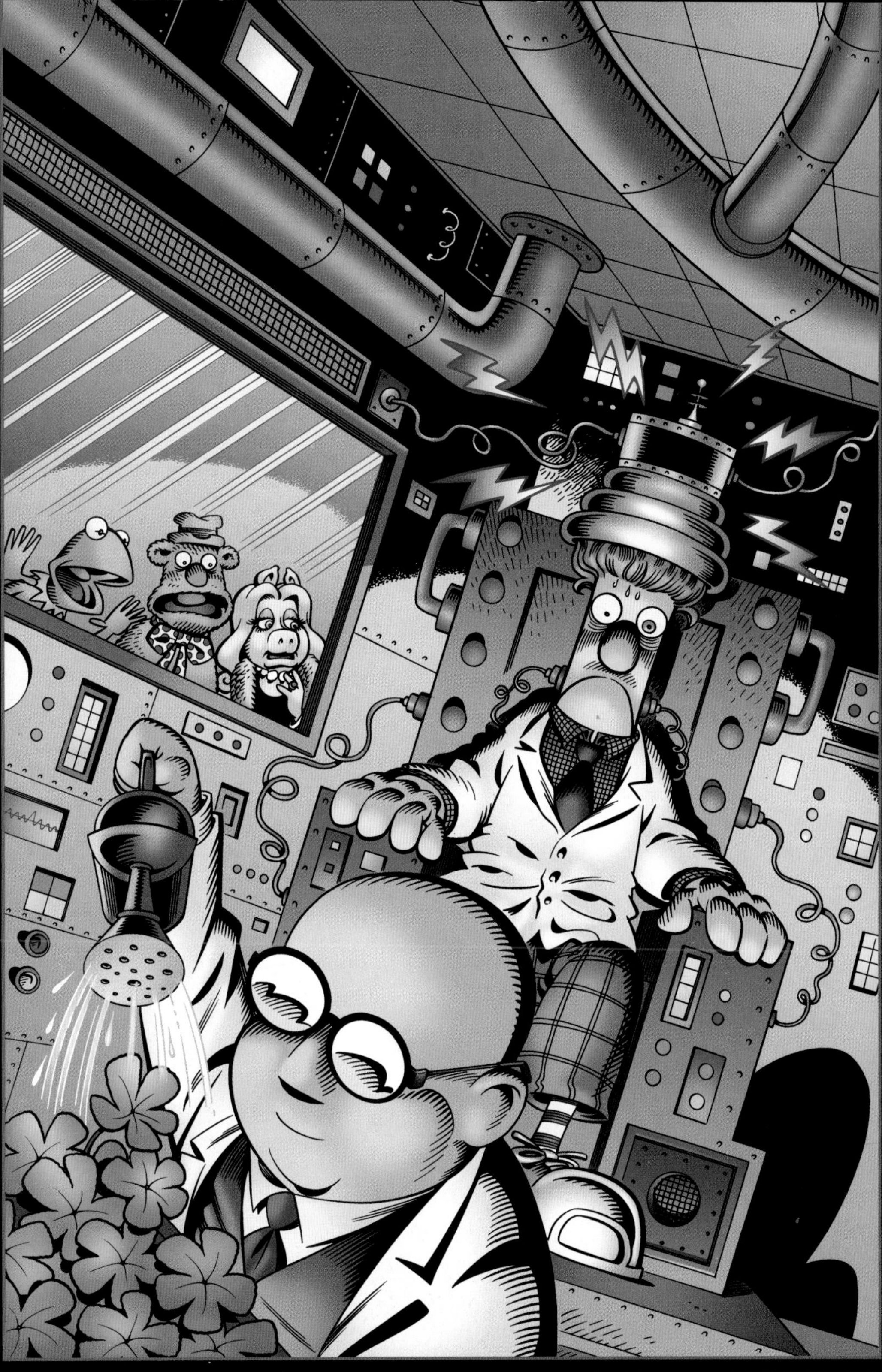

COVER 2B: ROGER LANGRIDGE

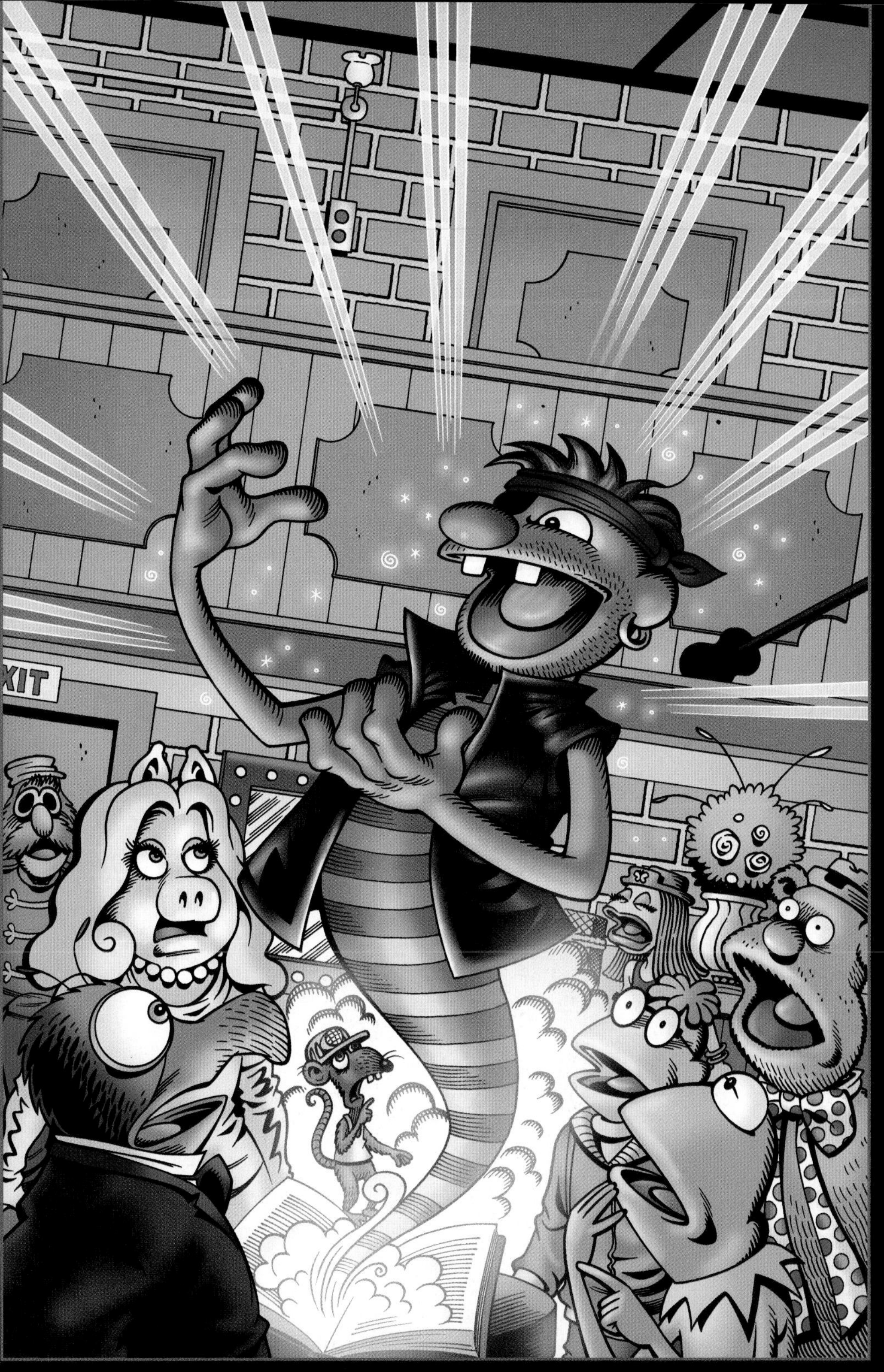

EXIT

COVER 4B: ROGER LANGRIDGE

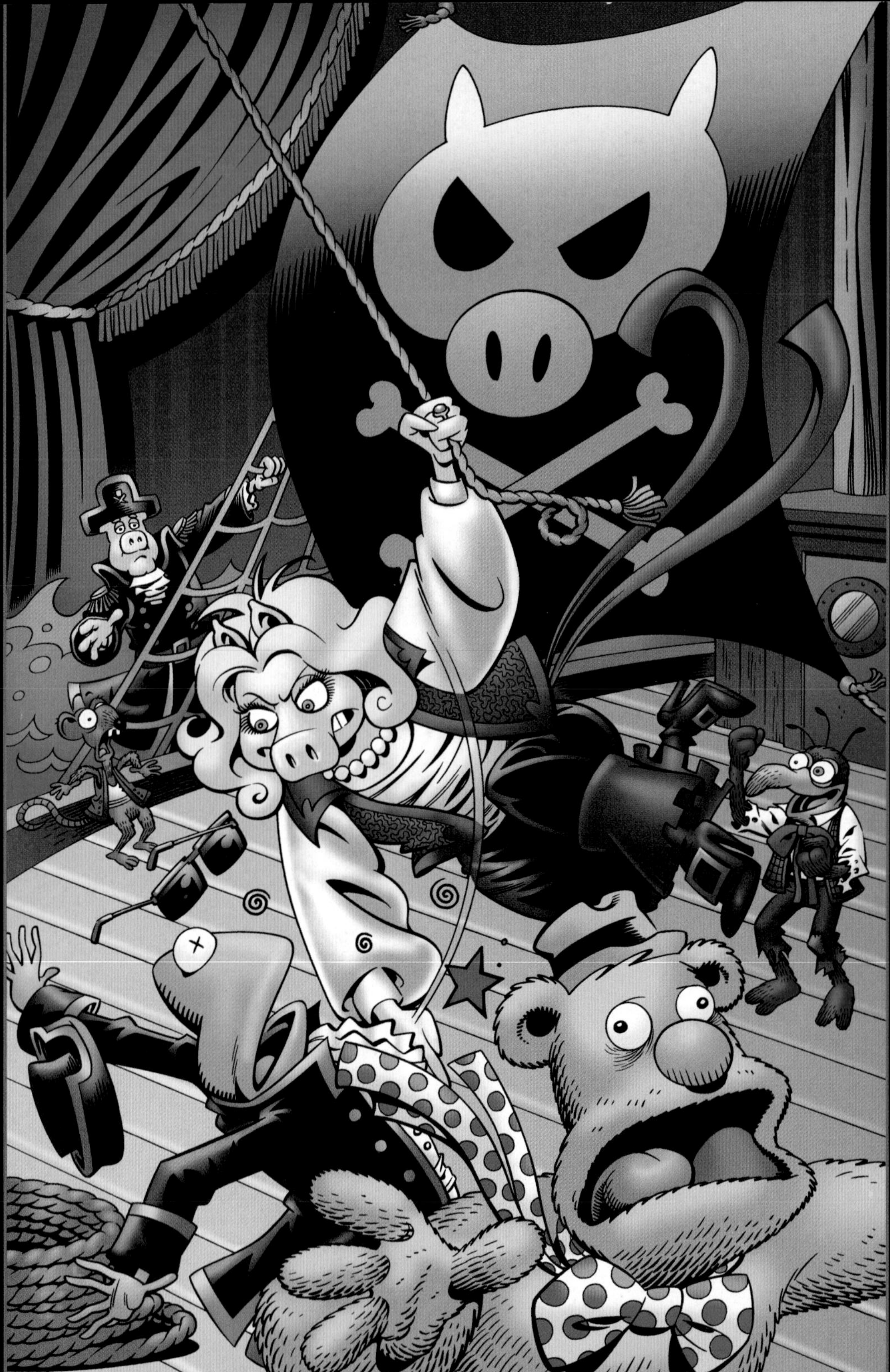

COVER 3B: ROGER LANGRIDGE

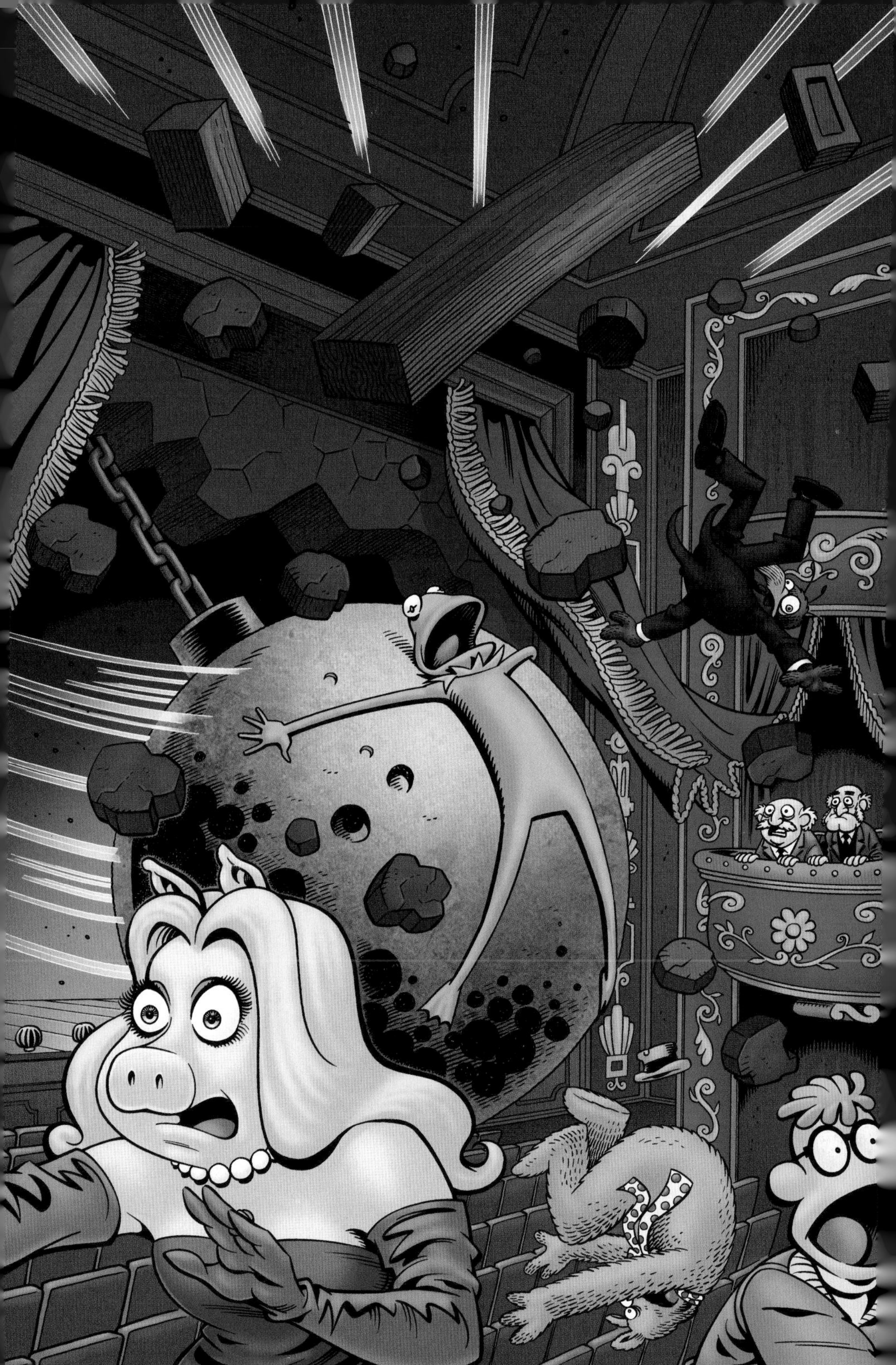

GER LANGRIDGE

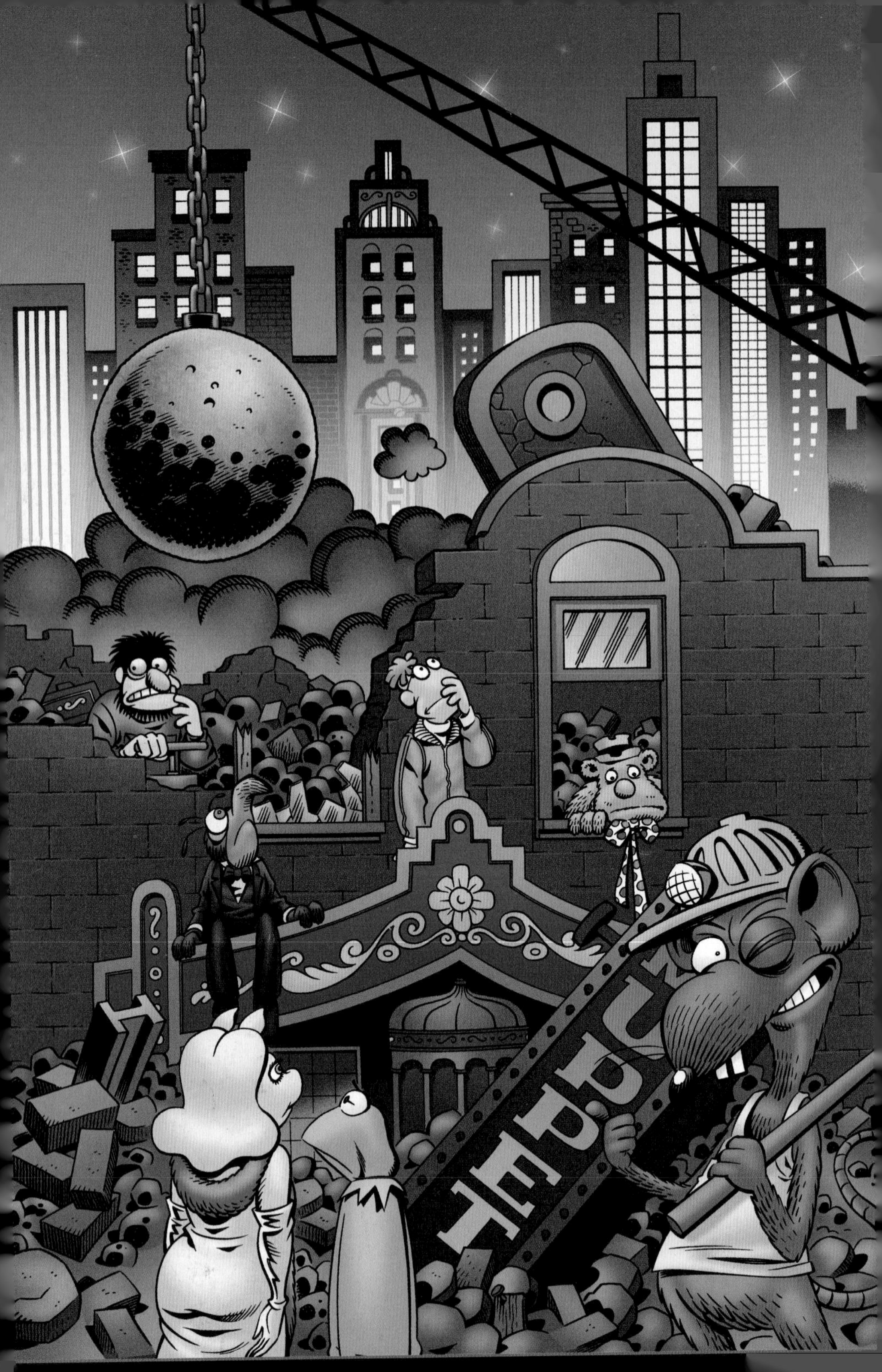

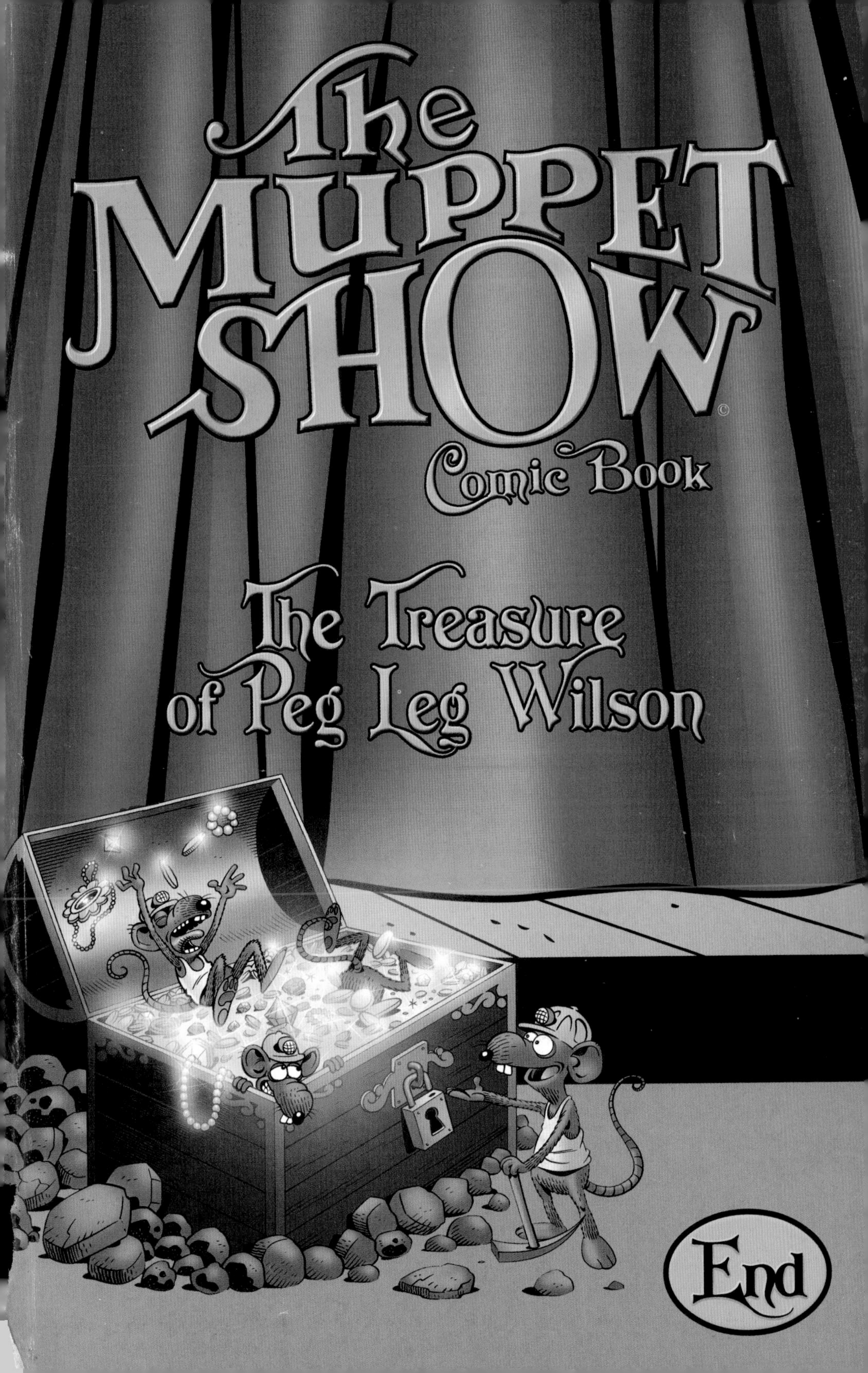
The MUPPET SHOW©
Comic Book
The Treasure of Peg Leg Wilson
End

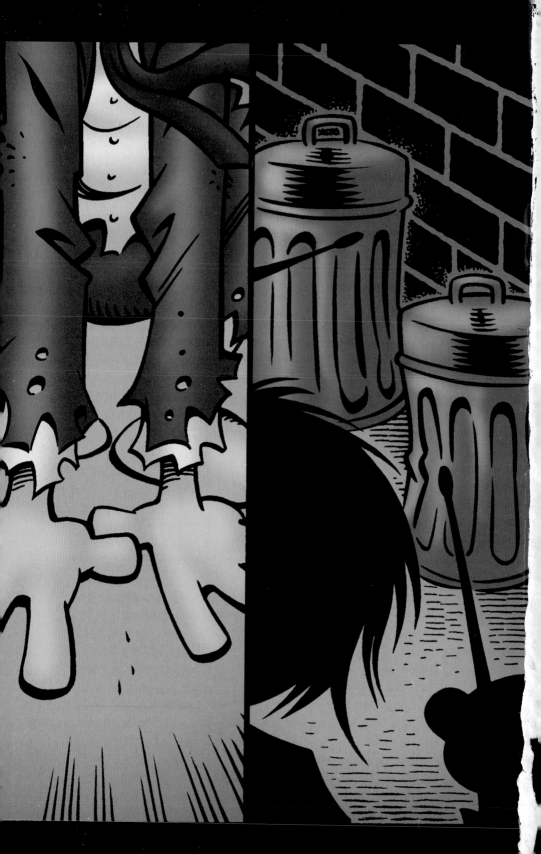

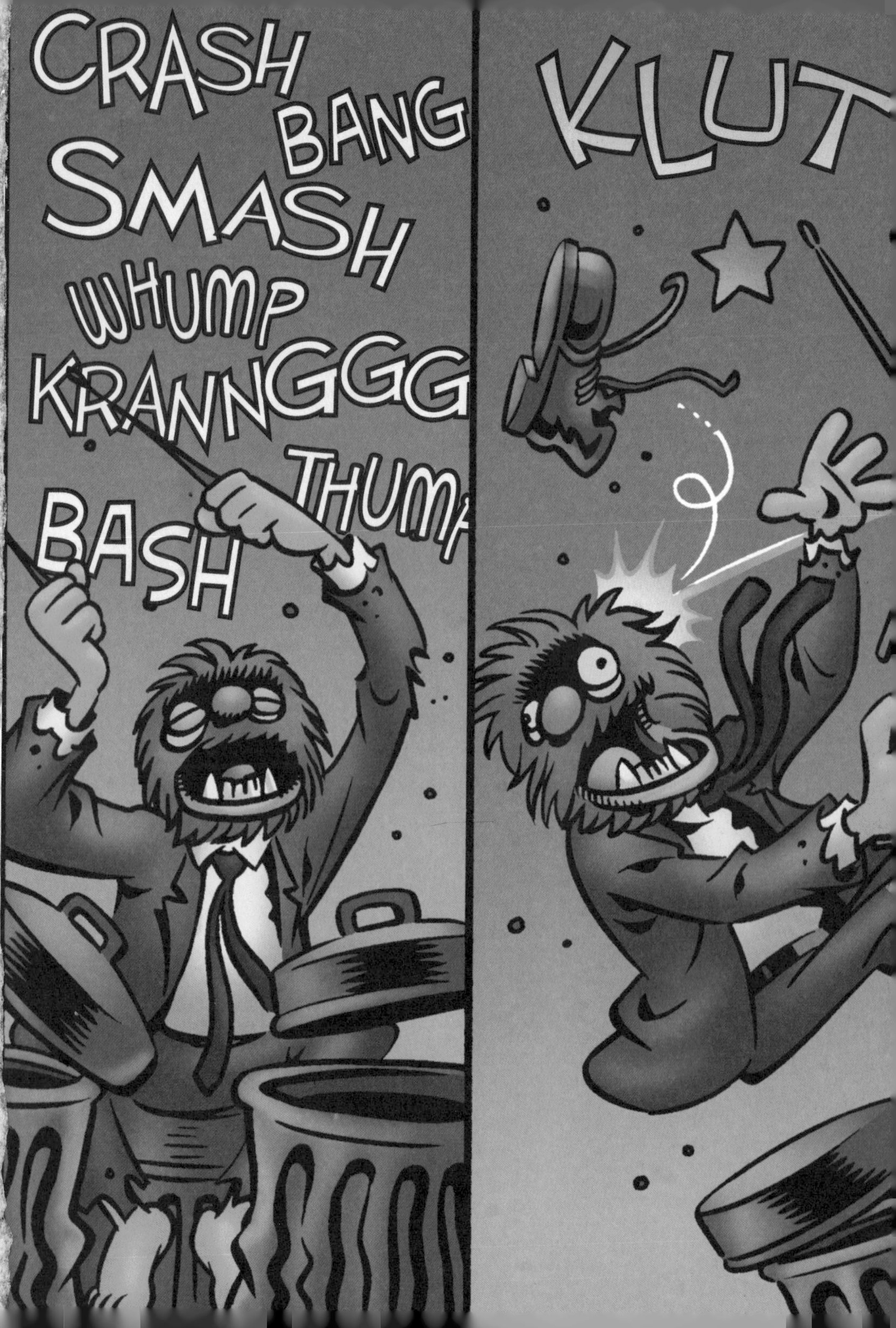
CRASH
BANG
SMASH
WHUMP
KRANNGGG
THUMP
BASH
KLUT